Ivy
and the
Meanstalk

Ivy
and the
Meanstalk

Dawn Lairamore

Holiday House / New York

Copyright © 2011 by Dawn Lairamore
All Rights Reserved
HOLIDAY HOUSE is registered in the U.S. Patent and Trademark Office.
Printed and Bound in August 2011 at Maple Vail, York, PA, USA.
www.holidayhouse.com
First Edition
1   3   5   7   9   10   8   6   4   2

Library of Congress Cataloging-in-Publication Data

Lairamore, Dawn.
Ivy and the meanstalk / by Dawn Lairamore.—1st American ed.
p. cm.
Summary: Fourteen-year-old Princess Ivy wants nothing more than to have a little
fun in the company of her dragon friend, Elridge, but unless she can recover the
magical harp snatched by a thieving youth named Jack long ago,
her entire kingdom will suffer an unspeakable fate.
ISBN 978-0-8234-2392-7 (hardcover)
[1. Fairy tales.   2. Princesses—Fiction.   3. Dragons—Fiction.   4. Giants—
Fiction.   5. Fairy godmothers—Fiction.]   1. Title.
PZ8.L1363Itm 2011
[Fic]—dc22
2010048627

 Contents

Part Three: The Burning Between and Back Again 165

Drusilla

Fairy Godmother to Her Royal Highness
Princess Ivory Isadora Imperia Irene
and

Boggs

Loyal Gatekeeper to His Royal Majesty
the King of Ardendale

request the pleasure of your esteemed
and otherworldly company as they celebrate

their most blissful and long-awaited union

on the most glorious twenty-third day of April
at eleven of the clock
Great Hall, Ardendale Castle, Kingdom of Ardendale

reception and refreshments to follow
in the magically enhanced castle gardens

Special Guest

Elridge

fierce and noble fire-breathing dragon

Dress—spare nothing

Weather—as perfect as fairy magic can make it

RSVP
by letter or carrier pigeon
(please indicate any food or flower allergies)

In lieu of presents (which are of course most welcome)
donations may be made to the Fairy Fashion Fund,
dedicated to providing appropriate finery
to the less fortunately dressed.

PART ONE

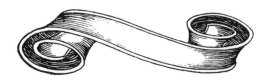

Gigantica

Wedding Day Woes

I'm starting to attract bees, Ivy thought ruefully, making shooing motions at the black-and-yellow speck buzzing in the air over her left shoulder. *I wish Drusilla hadn't insisted on an outdoor reception.*

Sighing heavily, the princess stared in dismay at the bulky bridesmaid dress weighing her down like a sack of sour apples, a dress that her deliriously happy fairy godmother had conjured up that very morning.

"I've had it planned for ages," Drusilla had gushed. "But I wanted it to be a surprise. I can't wait for you to see it. It's going to be the most beautiful bridesmaid dress ever!"

Unfortunately for Ivy, Drusilla's idea of "the most beautiful bridesmaid dress ever" was a huge, poufy gown made entirely of fresh flowers—roses, gardenias, orange blossoms, hyacinth, and a long sash of curly green vine heavy with honeysuckle. Drusilla had charmed the flowers so that they would remain fresh and sweet-smelling. As an added touch, the fairy had enchanted over a dozen white butterflies to flutter gracefully around the colorful collection of blossoms, so no matter where Ivy went, she was always at the center of a swarm of bugs.

Drusilla had nearly cried the first time she saw Ivy in the dress. She had said it was as lovely as a field of spring flowers. Ivy thought it was the most hideous thing she had ever seen, except for maybe the giant spider she had once gotten an extremely close look at when it had tried to eat her.

But Drusilla's worth it, the princess reminded herself, flooded with a mixture of fondness and resignation. *I want her to have the perfect wedding, even if it means having to wear this nightmare of a dress.*

One good thing about having the reception outdoors, besides the glorious spring weather, was that Elridge was able to attend. Elridge would have never fit inside the castle. While a relatively small dragon, he still was very nearly the size of the castle's gatehouse. But here in the castle garden, he could linger by Ivy's side and watch wedding guests dance to a lively tune played by a quartet of musicians.

"Mother sends her apologies for not coming," said Elridge, thumping his tail in time to the music, causing nearby flower-pots to jump every time it struck the ground. "She's still not very comfortable spending time in the valley." Ivy knew that Elridge's mother, the fearsome Dragon Queen, was still getting used to the idea that the humans of the valley kingdom of Ardendale were no longer her mortal enemies.

"Luckily, as the new Dragon Liaison to Ardendale, I can attend as her official representative," Elridge said proudly. Small and somewhat timid, Elridge had always been an embarrassment to the rest of the dragons who lived in the Smoke Sand Hills, even to his own mother. But since helping to bring peace between the humans and the dragons, and even learning to read, Elridge was now looked upon with a great deal of respect. He was extremely pleased when the Dragon Queen had seen fit to name him the official Dragon Liaison to Ardendale, especially as it gave him an excuse to spend even more time with his dear friend Ivy.

"Mother did send a goatskin gravy boat as a wedding gift for Drusy and Boggs. She's been saving it for a special occasion. Oh, dear me, you don't think they already have one, do you?" Elridge's scaly brow creased with concern.

"I'm pretty sure they don't," Ivy assured him, "although I wouldn't tell Toadstool what it's made from." She glanced over to where Drusilla's beloved pet pixie goat lounged on the sun-warmed stones of the garden walkway, eating stuffed mushrooms off a silver platter set out especially for her.

"No, of course not. Wouldn't want to upset her delicate sensibilities or anything like that," grumbled Elridge. Unlike normal goats, Toadstool had the gift of speech, a fact that Elridge often bemoaned, given how much the spoiled, bad-tempered creature complained.

Ivy's gaze drifted to the stretch of grass serving as a dance floor. "How come Drusilla gets an amazing dress while I'm stuck looking like I need to be pruned?" she asked wistfully. Her godmother, spinning with her new husband in the center of a circle of dancers, looked more beautiful than usual, if that was even possible. Her loose, snow-white hair shimmered like ice crystals in the spring sunshine. Her long, flowing gown was just as glittery, catching the light with diamond sparkles. The only spots of color against Drusilla's fair skin and white gown were her beautiful violet eyes. As always, she glowed with magic and light. Boggs, the castle's very aged—and very human—gatekeeper, was quite a contrast to his youthful fairy bride. He loved Drusilla dearly, however, and she was never happier than when showered with his affection.

"Look at the bright side. At least you smell like gardenias," said Elridge. "I love the smell of gardenias." The dragon leaned close and inhaled appreciatively. He promptly started coughing.

"Sorry...ugh, I think I just breathed in a butterfly." The dragon snorted loudly, and a white butterfly popped out of one of his melon-size nostrils. Startled, the butterfly fluttered in place for a moment before returning to its post, flitting around Ivy's fragrant gown.

"I wish Drusilla had told me what she had planned for my bridesmaid dress," complained the princess. "I would have tried to talk her out of it—or at least convince her to leave off the butterflies." She brushed at one of the pesky creatures fluttering so close to the side of her head that its wings tickled her ear. "But at least I had fun helping with the wedding arrangements." She broke into a sunny smile. "It took us weeks to get the menu just right. Drusilla was extremely particular. It drove Cook batty." The princess giggled at the memory of the castle cook throwing up her flour-dusted hands when Drusilla insisted that the fruit tarts be garnished with golden raspberries instead of red ones, to match the yellow peonies in her bridal bouquet. "But the food turned out wonderful, didn't it?"

"It *is* really good," Elridge agreed with enthusiasm. "I ate four roast pigeons, a rack of lamb, and two stuffed piglets all by myself.

And who knew liver could be so tasty? After today, I won't need to eat again for a week, maybe two." The dragon patted his belly contentedly. Now that he was spending time with humans, Elridge was branching out from the typical dragon's diet of wild goat. "Drusy probably shouldn't have pulled you from your studies so much, though," he said, his face suddenly serious. "Tildy was really upset that she had to postpone your geography lesson three times so you could help Drusy pick ribbon colors."

The princess felt a twinge of guilt at the mention of her nursemaid. "I know Tildy means well, but if she had it her way, I'd do nothing but study all day. Ever since Father said I was to inherit the throne, she hasn't given me a moment's peace." Ardendale had always been ruled by a king. Daughters didn't typically ascend the throne, but after Ivy—with Elridge's help—had saved the kingdom from certain destruction at the hands of an evil prince, her father had proclaimed her a worthy successor. "I don't understand why she gets her stockings in such a bunch." Ivy waved a hand dismissively, agitating two butterflies in the middle of circling her sleeve. "I can have lessons any old time. It's not every day that Drusilla gets married."

"But it isn't just wedding preparations that have been keeping you from your studies, is it," persisted Elridge. "What about last week, when you were supposed to read those north prickly pear confections, and we flew up to Cradle Lake to watch fidget flies instead?"

"The Prickly-Aldwin North Interkingdom Conventions," Ivy corrected, making a disagreeable face. "They're hundreds of pages long, Elridge, and all about boring stuff like peace alliances and interkingdom relations."

The corners of the dragon's mouth sagged in a guilty frown. "Still, I shouldn't have let you and Drusilla talk me into going. It could have waited until *after* you finished your assignment."

"Fidget flies only live for a few hours after they hatch. We would have missed the clouds of them dancing all over the lake if we had waited. And Drusilla hadn't seen fidget flies in over fourteen years. They don't have them on the Isle of Mist, you know." Drusilla had served as fairy godmother to the royal princesses of Ardendale for as long as anyone could remember. But her last goddaughter, Ivy's mother, had died when the princess was born, and Drusilla had been so overcome with guilt that she had fled the human world to the Isle of Mist, a magnificent, underground fairy kingdom. It seemed the perfect place to escape her grief. On the Isle of Mist, all fairies did was feast and celebrate. They never thought about anything unpleasant, and their biggest worry was when the next party would be. It was only six months ago, shortly after Ivy's fourteenth birthday, that Drusilla had left this frivolous existence and returned to Ardendale to resume her role as Ivy's fairy godmother and reunite with her true love, Boggs.

"Fidget flies dance every year," Elridge said matter-of-factly. "It's not like this was her last chance to see them." A furrow formed between his eyes. "Drusilla really should do more to encourage your studies. I know fairies like to enjoy themselves, but life isn't all fun and games."

"At least Drusilla knows how to have fun," retorted Ivy, thinking perhaps Elridge's new post as Dragon Liaison to Ardendale might be going to his head. "Lately, all everyone else does is throw lessons and lectures at me."

She hoped Elridge would pick up on her not-so-subtle hint,

but the dragon plowed on, undeterred. "I don't know why you hate studying so much, anyway. You love books. You were the one who taught me to read."

"I love *stories*," corrected the princess, exasperated. "Tales, adventures, exciting things. Interkingdom conventions hardly make for riveting reading."

"Well, you have to admit, Tildy has a point. If you're going to rule Ardendale one day, there are important things you need to know."

"You're starting to sound just like her," muttered Ivy. "You worry too much, Elridge. It's Drusilla's wedding day. We should be enjoying ourselves." She gave the dragon her most pleading look, pouting pathetically and blinking up at him imploringly. It was a look that had always worked on her father when she was small. "Pleeeeease?"

Elridge tried very hard to hold his stern expression, but the corners of his mouth twitched. Then his face split into a toothy grin. "Oh, all right," he said with a good-natured laugh. "But please stop making that ridiculous face."

2

A Visitor at the Gate

"**H**ullo, Ivy."

The princess turned toward the friendly voice and found the castle's stocky stable boy, Owen, strolling up from the opposite end of the garden. She was surprised by how nice he looked, his clothes clean and his curly red hair neatly combed for once. Usually, Owen was busy working in the stables and was covered in dirt and hay.

Ivy realized she was still making the silly, pouty face that she had given Elridge. Horrified, she quickly sucked in her lower lip and tried to act casual. "Oh hello, Owen," she said breezily.

Elridge glanced back and forth between the princess and the stable boy with a strange expression on his long, reptilian face. He suddenly seemed a bit embarrassed to be there.

"Um…I think I'm going to…uh, get a piece of that delicious-looking cake. Yes, that's it—a nice piece of cake." The dragon hurried off in the direction of Drusilla's five-tiered white wedding cake, which was the size and shape of a large fountain. Vanilla sauce actually spouted from the top and flowed down the sides in white cascades.

"It was a nice ceremony," Owen said in a cheerful voice. "I've never seen Drusilla glow so brightly, and Boggs has been grinning like a barn cat getting his belly scratched all day." Two rosy spots suddenly appeared high on the stable boy's cheeks, the color very nearly matching his hair. "And you...you look very..."

Ivy shifted, suddenly feeling sillier than ever. "Foolish? Absurd? Ridiculous beyond words?"

"I was going to say flowery." Owen laughed. "Really, Ivy, the dress isn't that bad."

"Easy for you to say. You don't look like a walking shrub." The princess sighed. "But don't say anything to Drusilla. I told her I loved it." Ivy let her eyes wander to the dance floor once more. "And I really shouldn't complain. I mean, Drusilla and Boggs do look really happy, don't they. Drusilla was thrilled to finally have a wedding. Do you know she's been engaged twenty-four times?"

Owen looked stunned. "Really?"

"Well, Drusilla *is* hundreds of years old," said Ivy. "And you know how much bad luck she's had when it comes to relationships." The princess thought of how her godmother was always spouting off about her countless failed romances. Ivy caught Owen's eye, and they both burst out laughing.

"All kidding aside, I think you look very nice." Owen shuffled his ungainly feet. "I'd ask you to dance, but I'm not sure I could put my arms around you without squashing a couple of poor butterflies."

Ivy didn't know what to say. The idea of Owen's arms around her was alarming and yet, at the same time, just the tiniest bit...nice. She flushed with embarrassment. "I'm a lousy dancer, anyway."

"Me too," said Owen. He cleared his throat uncomfortably. "Maybe Elridge has the right idea. Want to get some cake?"

Relieved, Ivy agreed at once. The two of them made for the banquet table near the boxwood hedge, passing Toadstool on the garden walkway. The tiny goat immediately released a volley of squeaky sneezes.

"Didn't I tell you not to come near me in that dress?" she whined in her nasally voice, shooting the princess a nasty look. She had a golden bow around her neck for the occasion, but the look on her stubby face was anything but festive. "You know I can't tolerate dirt—or anything that grows in it." Up until six months ago, Toadstool had lived with Drusilla on the Isle of Mist, where everything was made of quartz and crystal, even the trees. She hadn't taken well to the "dirty" green world above-ground. "I just stopped sneezing from all the grass out here— why anyone would put grass in a garden is beyond me—and now you've gone and made my eyes water and my nose get all drippy again." She sniffled intensely, as if to prove how much distress she was really in.

"Sorry," said Ivy, and she and Owen hurried away from the querulous little goat as quickly as possible.

Elridge was chewing on a large chunk of wedding cake—one whole tier, from the look of it. Ivy's friends Rose and Clarinda were at the banquet table, too, but they had considerably smaller slices. Rose looked lovely in a dress of dark blue, with matching ribbons in her golden curls. The dark-haired, soft-spoken Clarinda looked equally fetching in lace-trimmed mauve.

"Oh good," said Rose, bubbly with her usual high spirits. "We were about to sit down and eat our cake. You're just in time to join us."

"I don't think Ivy *can* sit in that dress," Clarinda said, eyeing the princess's gown with concern. "All the flowers on the back will be crushed. Probably some butterflies, too."

"I didn't think about that." Ivy groaned. "Great, I'll just have to stand for the rest of the day. And my feet are already killing me." Drusilla had magically enlarged two lady slipper orchids for Ivy to wear. They were terribly uncomfortable; pebbles poked straight through the delicate bottoms and into the princess's feet.

Elridge swallowed a mouthful of cake so large that Ivy could see a bulge travel down his throat. "Maybe you can lean against a tree," he suggested, licking vanilla sauce off one of his claws. "Just with one shoulder—very carefully."

"And maybe we shouldn't stand so close to you," said Rose, glancing down at her plate. "A butterfly almost got stuck in the icing on my cake—and here comes another bee!"

For about the hundredth time that day, Ivy wished she were wearing something normal.

"Ivory! Princess Ivory!" A voice cut through the crowd as sharply as a brass bell. Ivy knew its source at once. Tildy was the only person who ever called her by her full name.

"There you are!" The nursemaid swept up from the direction of the castle. Her plump form was draped in a periwinkle gown, and her graying hair was neatly pinned to the back of her head. Ivy caught a whiff of the lavender water she always washed in. "I need you to run and fetch your godmother," she commanded in a rather pinched tone. "There is a man asking for her at the castle gate."

"For Drusilla?" Ivy was puzzled. "But it's the middle of her wedding reception. Are you sure he isn't looking for someone else?"

"Quite sure," Tildy replied testily. "Only your godmother would know someone this odd." Tildy thought Drusilla was as flighty as fairy dust and only tolerated her because she was Ivy's godmother. "He looks rather...frazzled. Thinks he can just show up in the middle of a wedding reception and insist upon seeing the bride. Really, some people have no sense of propriety! He's clearly not a man of breeding. Best get Drusilla out there before he stirs up any trouble. I asked him to wait outside the castle gate, just to be safe. He said Drusilla would know him," Tildy continued primly. "His name is Gizzle the Green."

Gizzle the Green

When Drusilla heard the visitor's name, her fair face went even paler than usual.

"Gizzy, here?" Her normally lovely bell-like voice sounded tight and strained. "But...how? Why? I mean, I haven't seen hide nor hair of that maddening mage in centuries, and then he just shows up out of the blue on my wedding day. Did he say what he wants?" Her violet eyes were as wide as medallions. She seemed nervous—frightened even—which was most unlike her. Ivy had seen her fairy godmother stare down the ferocious Dragon Queen without batting a beautiful eyelash.

"I don't know what he wants," Ivy said. "I figured he was a friend of yours."

"No," said Drusilla, a little too quickly. "Not a friend, exactly...although he and I were once close...a very, very long time ago." She looked away guiltily.

"He's one of your old sweethearts!" Ivy exclaimed, a little louder than she had intended.

"*Shhhhhh.* Keep your voice down," Drusilla hissed, lowering her own to an urgent whisper. She shot a furtive glance toward the dance floor. Boggs was out there, enjoying a waltz with one of the serving girls from the castle kitchen. "Oh, this could be a huge disaster. I hope Gizzy's not here to ruin my wedding day. We didn't exactly part on good terms." Drusilla moaned and buried her face in her hands. "And he wasn't just a sweetheart. We were supposed to get married."

Ivy drew a sharp breath. "What happened?"

"Gizzle's job is very important to him," Drusilla said bitterly, lifting her head. "He said he loved me, yet he spent more time at work than he did with me. I called off the wedding. I bet he's still angry. He always was the type to hold a grudge. What if he makes a scene in front of my guests? My beautiful wedding will be ruined. Oh Ivy, what am I going to do?" Drusilla's violet eyes were bright; she looked ready to cry.

"You have to talk to him," said Ivy, laying a comforting hand on her godmother's shoulder. "We can't just leave him standing outside the castle gate. Besides, maybe he dropped by to say hello because he just happened to be in the neighborhood." She tried to keep her tone light, but the words sounded unconvincing even to her. Ardendale was an isolated valley. No one ever "just happened to be in the neighborhood."

"Yes, you're right, of course. I'm sure it's no big deal." Drusilla took a steadying breath, then she lunged forward and seized one of Ivy's hands in both of her own, gazing at the princess with large, pleading eyes. "Ivy, come with me? I don't think I can face Gizzy alone."

Ivy swallowed with difficulty. She had heard enough of Drusilla's stories to know that a good number of her godmother's old suitors were ... well, *odd* was the only word for it. Wizards, weather warlocks, knights errant, monarchs, fairy fire mages, mimes, and mortals of rather dubious natures—including pirates and spice smugglers—had all courted Drusilla at one time or another. She wasn't sure that she wanted to meet one of them, but she didn't have the heart to say no.

"Of course," she said, pushing her reluctance aside.

"Oh, thank you, Ivy," gushed Drusilla, still clinging to her hand like a miser to his last coin. "Thank you, thank you, thank you."

Ivy gave her godmother a reassuring smile. "Everything will be fine," she said, "you'll see."

Once the princess set eyes on Gizzle the Green, however, she wasn't so sure.

Tildy hadn't been exaggerating when she said the man outside the castle gate looked frazzled. Long mousy hair hung about his face like a curtain, with the stub of a nose poking through the part in the middle. It did a poor job of hiding the sorry state of his face, for through the greasy strands of hair Ivy could see scratches on his pale cheeks and a purple bruise beneath one eye. His green robes were torn, and his calloused hands clung to a twisted ash-wood staff. Ivy blinked, for before her eyes the staff was sprouting, shooting out twigs, branches, and leaves that grew larger and larger, all stretching out as if to caress the man's battered face.

"Drusilla," he said, eyes lighting up as he caught sight of Ivy and her godmother approaching the gate. He limped forward to meet them, leaning heavily on his staff. As the edges of his robes pulled away from his mud-splattered boots, Ivy could see a crescent-shaped scar on his left leg. It was a strange wound, made up of what looked like dozens of little punctures. Judging from the still-oozing scabs, the injury was fairly recent.

"Gizzy," Drusilla replied, forcing a smile. "How nice to see you after all this time."

"Yes," agreed the man. "What's it been—eight, nine hundred years?"

"Something like that," said Drusilla.

"You're looking as lovely as ever," he remarked, taking in the fine figure she cut in her dazzling white wedding dress.

"Thanks," said Drusilla, shifting uncomfortably. "And you look... um... well." She purposely averted her eyes from his torn robes and bloody leg.

The branches on the man's staff had now grown so long, it looked as if he were holding a small sapling. Leaves were stroking his face lovingly.

"*Pfffft.*" He spit away a cluster that brushed against his lips. "Get off me, you deciduous delinquent."

It was then that Ivy heard a rustling sound and noticed a strange tugging sensation come over her body. Looking down, she saw that the hundreds of flowers on her dress had turned their tiny heads toward the man, stretching and straining as if desperate to reach out and touch him. The honeysuckle sash at her waist actually started to grow, until the green ends reached the ground and snaked out toward him. The butterflies were greatly alarmed; they flapped their wings wildly, but Drusilla's charm held them firmly in place.

"Sorry about that," said the man, noticing the effect he was having. "Plants can sense sources of green magic. They're quite drawn to me. Gets a bit bothersome sometimes." He slapped away another affectionate branch.

"This is my goddaughter, Ivy," said Drusilla.

"Ivy." The man nodded approvingly. "*Hedera helix.* Fine ornamental climber."

"If you say so," said Drusilla. She turned to the princess. "Ivy, meet Gizzle the Green. He's from the North Continent. He's Assistant Head Plant Mage at the Blooming Brightly Institute of Magical Flora."

"*Former* Assistant Head Plant Mage at the Blooming Brightly Institute of Magical Flora," Gizzle corrected. He drew himself to his full height and puffed out his chest importantly. "I struck out on my own some time ago. Nothing new or exciting ever happened at B.B.I.M.F., what with that bunch of flower-happy old biddies running the place. All they ever wanted to do was cultivate new varieties of magical flowers: magical *Bellis perennis*, magical *Lathyrus odoratus*, magical *Convallaria maja-lis.* And don't get me started on the magical marigolds. I mean, really, how many types of enchanted *Tagetes patula* does the world really need? I wasn't about to squander any more of my precious time growing marigolds that sparkled or blew bubbles. I had far more important work that needed my attention."

By this time, the vine at Ivy's waist had grown almost long enough to touch the edge of Gizzle's tattered robe.

"Fine specimen of *Lonicera periclymenum*," he said, glancing down at it. He eyed the rest of Ivy's dress critically. "Would you like me to give you something to take care of that nasty infestation?"

"I conjured up those butterflies, and I think they're beauti-ful!" Drusilla's voice tightened with indignation.

"Oh yes—of course they are," Gizzle said hurriedly. "Very lovely."

But Drusilla seemed to have lost all patience for niceties. "So Gizzle, what brings you to Ardendale—on my wedding day?" she asked bluntly.

It was Gizzle's turn to look uncomfortable. "Well, I know things didn't end very well between us," he said, "and I figured it was time to bury the hatchet. Not long ago, I visited the Isle of Mist. I heard from some of your fairy friends that you were getting married, so I thought I'd stop by to offer my congratulations and let you know that I forgive you for... for... for breaking our engagement and tossing me aside like some lowly weed you yanked from the garden of your heart." The corner of his bruised eye started to twitch, and Ivy couldn't help thinking that he didn't sound very forgiving at all. "I mean," he added quickly, "for things not working out between us." He fumbled in the pockets of his robe and drew out a loop of multicolored beads. "I even brought you a little present, just to show there are no hard feelings."

"That was sweet of you, Gizzy," said Drusilla, looking hugely relieved.

"It's a necklace," said the plant mage. "I made it myself."

Drusilla examined the small beaded necklace with interest. "These beads look familiar," she said. "I think I've seen something like them before."

"No, you haven't," snapped Gizzle. "Wh-what I mean is, those beads are very, very rare."

Drusilla slipped the strand onto her delicate neck. "Thank you, Gizzy," she said. "Would you like to come into the garden for a slice of wedding cake?"

"No, thank you," said Gizzle. "I must be off. I have important work waiting for me. It was nice seeing you again, Drusilla." He turned to leave, but Ivy's honeysuckle sash had coiled tightly around his ankle. The princess had to give it several solid tugs before it finally let go. With a brief nod of good-bye, Gizzle turned and hobbled toward the road. It was slow going, between his limp and the fact that his staff was now the size of a small tree. Branches were starting to wrap around his neck, choking him in a leafy hug. He had to stop to pry them off before continuing.

"Gizzy always was all work and no play," said Drusilla. "I don't know what I ever saw in him...although he did bring me the most beautiful flowers. For the record, I really like magical marigolds." She watched Gizzle's retreating form thoughtfully. "His work must be a lot more exciting these days. He never used to get roughed up like that at B.B.I.M.F."

Ivy hadn't cared for the moody little plant mage and was glad he was gone. The flowers on her dress had finally settled down. She turned to walk back to the castle garden with her godmother, being careful not to trip over her honeysuckle sash, which trailed behind her like a curly green kite string.

"You were right, Ivy," said Drusilla, as they entered the garden. "That wasn't nearly as bad as I expected. I even got a gift for all my trouble, although these beads don't go very well with my wedding dress, do they?"

Ivy leaned over to examine the necklace. "If it weren't for all the strange colors, I'd say they looked like beans," she said.

"It would be just like Gizzy to use beans to make jewelry," said Drusilla, rolling her violet eyes. "He always did have all sorts of seeds and shoots lying around."

They passed Toadstool, still lounging on the stone walkway with her eyes closed. Her platter of mushrooms was empty, her belly was bloated, and her mouth curved in a satisfied smile. The ribbon around her neck was half undone, the ends stained with juniper sauce.

"Oh Toady-Woady, your pretty ribbon is ruined," cried Drusilla. She quickly bent and pulled it free. Slipping off Gizzle's necklace, she fastened it around the goat's little neck like a collar. "There, it looks much better on you, my lovely little darling." The fairy leaned down and planted a kiss on top of the goat's bristly white head.

Toadstool was so comfortable and content, she didn't even crack an eye.

Toadstool Takes a Trip

"What was that all about?" asked Elridge, when Ivy rejoined the dragon, Owen, Rose, and Clarinda by the banquet table, which was noticeably less laden than when she had left it. "And what happened to your dress?" Ivy had had to wind the honeysuckle sash around her waist four times and tie the ends in a knot to keep it from dragging along the ground.

"I'll tell you later," said the princess. Across the garden, she could see her father, the king, rising to give the wedding toast, silver goblet in hand.

"My dear friends," he addressed the crowd, blue eyes twinkling above his tumble of gray beard. "Those of you who have known Boggs and Drusilla for as long as I have no doubt realize what a truly special day this is. Their love was strong and true enough to endure a most unfortunate separation, and their happy union is here at last." His gaze wandered to where Drusilla stood holding hands with her husband under a flowering lilac tree. In the nearly fourteen years she had been gone, time had transformed Boggs into an old man. The eternally youthful Drusilla, however, still looked as young and radiant as ever, despite being hundreds of years old. "I, for one, am beyond delighted that they have reunited," said the king. "And while there are those who say May-December marriages never work, I have no concerns about the age difference. I know Drusilla is more than capable of keeping up with a much younger man." He winked at the smiling couple as a titter ran through the crowd. Then he raised his goblet high. "I hope all of you will join me in wishing the bride and groom a future rich in happiness. May they cherish each other al—"

A harsh sound interrupted the king's speech. Toadstool, still lying on her side on the garden walkway, had begun to make choking noises, which were growing louder by the moment. The little goat struggled to her feet and stumbled onto the grass.

"Toadstool, darling, what's wrong?" Drusilla was across the garden in a sparkling white flash, falling to her knees next to the troubled goat.

"Probably got a fur ball stuck in her throat and wants someone to hold her hoof while she coughs it up," Elridge muttered to Ivy. "You know she always has to be the center of attention."

But Ivy couldn't help thinking that, for once, the little goat wasn't merely making a scene. She looked to be in true distress, her tawny eyes bulging as if ready to burst out of her stubby face like two overripe berries under the summer sun.

"Do you have something caught in your throat?" Drusilla laid a loving hand on the pixie goat's back. "Toady-Woady, darling, tell me what's wrong." She leaned down for a closer look.

"Oh!" she cried, panic filling her voice. "She's starting to turn blue! I don't think she can breathe. Boggs, Ivy, help—it's that necklace!"

Ivy glanced at the beaded necklace encircling the goat's neck and was startled to see that the rainbow-colored beads were swelling, growing larger and larger, tightening dangerously around poor Toadstool's tiny throat.

"I can't get it off," cried Drusilla, tugging desperately.

Ivy raced to help. The beads were now almost the size of quail eggs. Their surfaces started to split, and Ivy caught flashes of green. Before the princess could reach Toadstool, a long, twisting tendril burst from one of the beads, shattering it with a pop. The string snapped, and beads scattered like pebbles in the grass at Toadstool's feet. More tendrils burst forth, burrowing deep into the rich garden soil.

Then the ground began to rumble. Ivy struggled to stay on her feet as the earth beneath her heaved.

"Whoa—what's going on?" cried Elridge. Even the dragon was being tossed like a boat on a stormy sea.

"Earthquake!" someone shouted. Cries of alarm rose from the gathered guests, and many dashed for the shelter of the castle.

The rumbling grew louder, and a mound of earth rose where the beads had fallen. A massive green stalk, as big around as the miller's grindstone, erupted from its core. Toadstool, at the center of the scattered beads, found herself sitting atop the giant stalk as it shot skyward at blinding speed.

"Drusyyyyyyyyyyyyy!" cried the little goat as she was carried away.

"Toadstool!" screamed Drusilla. "Toadstool—no!"

But the ground continued to shake, and the enormous stalk continued to climb. Tendrils twined around it like slithering snakes. Heart-shaped leaves larger than elephant ears burst from the twisted trunk, as well as fat, puffy pods the size of pillows.

"Stay back!" the king shouted over the clamor, ushering what was left of the crowd away from the leafy column. "Everyone stay back!"

Just as Ivy began to think the stalk would grow forever, the towering trunk lurched to a stop. Many in the crowd went tumbling as the earth beneath their feet unexpectedly stilled.

For a moment, stunned silence hung over the garden. Then Drusilla's sobs rent the air.

"Oh, my poor Toadstool," she wailed, burying her face in her hands. "My poor, poor Toadstool!"

"Good goat fur," said Elridge, teetering back and forth as he struggled to regain his balance. "What just happened? What *is* that thing?"

"I...I think it's a beanstalk," said Owen. He nodded at the green pods. There were hundreds of them up and down the length of the giant trunk. "Those kind of look like the bean pods in my mother's vegetable garden, only squatter and puffier. And bigger," he added, rather unnecessarily. "A whole lot bigger."

Cautiously, Ivy and her friends moved to the foot of the stalk, where Drusilla was still crying grievously. Boggs had wrapped a comforting arm around his wife's shoulders and was clutching her to his chest. Drusilla looked faded, her usual glow dulled by her distress.

"I w-wish my magic were s-stronger," she bawled. "Then I c-could do s-something. I could w-whisk Toadstool b-back with some sort of s-spell." Being a fairy godmother, Drusilla was proficient at small spells and charms, especially those of a domestic nature, but her magic wasn't nearly powerful enough to deal with a giant beanstalk in the middle of the castle garden. "Oh, th-this is all m-my fault. If only I hadn't p-put that stupid n-necklace on Toadstool, she w-would still be here. I h-have to do something... I h-have to save—*hic*—"

"Ow!" Boggs jumped back from his wife as white sparks exploded from the top of her head. Several smoked and sizzled as they landed on his linen tunic, and one burned a hole in the toe of his boot. "Drusy, love, are you okay?" he asked, eyeing her with concern. "You just... sparked."

"Sorry," Drusilla said in a helpless voice that made her sound like a very small child. Sniffling, she wiped her eyes. "This sometimes happens when I get upset—*hic*—" All the roses on a nearby bush turned into frilly red frogs, who burst into a chorus of croaks and hopped off in every direction. "I get a bad case of the hiccups and can't control my magic—*hic*—" A member of the King's Guard, standing close by, suddenly had hair that was bright blue, which would have been quite unfortunate if it hadn't perfectly matched his blue livery.

Drusilla stomped her foot in frustration. "Fairy cakes, I don't have time for this—*hic*—" The morning glory vines climbing the trellis behind her transformed into eels and fell to the ground in a wriggling heap. "I have to get up that beanstalk—*hic*—" A silver punch bowl on the banquet table sprouted wings.

"I'm not sure that's such a good idea, love," said Boggs, who watched his wife worriedly but was leery enough not to put his arms around her again.

"Of course, I'm not thinking straight," said Drusilla, observing the punch bowl flutter away. "Elridge, you have wings—*hic*—" A mermaid topiary burst into a beautiful aria, gesturing dramatically as she sang in a flawless soprano. "You could fly me to the top of the beanstalk—*hic*—" All of the leaves on a nearby tree incinerated on the spot, leaving nothing but a smoldering pile of ash.

"I'm not flying her anywhere," Elridge muttered to the princess under his breath. "Not when she's like this. She's likely to turn my wings into lace doilies—and it'd be a long way down for the both of us."

"Drusilla, I really don't think you're in any condition to fly," Ivy told her godmother gently.

"Nonsense, I'm perfectly fine," insisted Drusilla, placing her hands on her hips. "And I have to find Toadstool—*hic*—"

There was a bang like a canon being fired as what was left of Drusilla's enormous wedding cake exploded. Icing and vanilla sauce rained down upon the startled guests. Some let out shrieks and ran from the garden. Others just stood there looking shocked, coated from head to toe in dripping, sticky white.

Drusilla gasped and clamped a hand over her mouth. Her violet eyes were bright. She looked as if she might start to cry again.

"Look—don't worry. Elridge and I will fly to the top of the beanstalk and rescue Toadstool," said Ivy, hoping to calm her godmother before anything else exploded.

Beside her, Elridge grimaced. "I knew you were going to say that."

Drusilla cautiously uncovered her lips, hope shining in her gemlike eyes. "Really? You'd do that for me?"

"Of course," said Ivy, squeezing her godmother's arm warmly. "You're family, and that makes Toadstool family, too."

Drusilla seemed to regain a little of her glow. For the first time in several minutes, she was able to speak without dissolving into hiccups.

"Oh, Ivy," she said. "Please hurry, before anything happens to her. My poor little Toadstool is probably frightened out of her mind."

"Yes," muttered Elridge, so quietly that only the princess could hear. "There's no one to serve her stuffed mushrooms and rub her belly at the top of a giant beanstalk."

Ivy shot him a reproving look before scrambling onto his back, which was a bit difficult in her bridesmaid outfit. The delicate lady slipper orchids tore on the edges of Elridge's scales. Petals fell from her gown in a soft shower, and the butterflies became quite discombobulated, finding it difficult to flutter around Ivy's dress as she climbed.

She finally managed to position herself between two of the thick spines that ran along the ridge of Elridge's back, the fit uncomfortably snug, the full skirts of her gown ballooning up around her.

"Are you sure this is safe, Ivy?" asked her father, who had joined the group at the base of the beanstalk.

Owen, too, looked nervous. "Maybe I should go with you."

Ivy flushed with pleasure at his concern but forced herself to shake her head. "A straight flight is one thing, but that's a steep climb." The arduous flight was going to be rough on Elridge, and they had no idea how high the stalk extended. "The more passengers Elridge carries, the more it will slow him down. We need to reach Toadstool as quickly as possible."

Both her father and Owen still looked doubtful.

"Don't worry," Ivy told them. "It's just a big beanstalk. We'll fly to the top, pick up Toadstool, and fly back down. What could possibly go wrong?"

5

In the Clouds

Elridge followed the stalk like a green trail through the sky, circling its towering trunk as he soared higher and higher. The white butterflies around Ivy's dress flapped furiously, but there was no way they could keep pace. One by one, they fell back and were left behind, hovering in the air as if unsure what to do. The dress itself held up better than Ivy expected, although a fair number of petals floated to earth in the wake of the speeding dragon.

"That man at the castle gate—Gizzle the Green—gave Drusilla those beads," Ivy told him as he pumped his wings. "I *thought* they looked like beans." She clutched the spine in front of her tightly. From here, the castle looked about the size of a child's toy block. A bank of white clouds hung over their heads, drawing closer with every flap of Elridge's scalloped wings. It was a good thing Ivy wasn't bothered by heights. The top of the beanstalk was still nowhere in sight. "Gizzle is a plant mage. You don't think he knew this would happen, do you?"

"Knew those beans would sprout into a monster beanstalk?" Elridge sounded shocked. "Why would he give something like that to Drusilla?"

"I don't know," admitted Ivy. "But something about him seemed a bit off. I think we'd better be careful, just in case."

The dragon sighed forlornly. "Dear me, why do we always end up flying into trouble?"

His long body pierced the cloud bank, the world below lost from view as they were swallowed by a sea of white. The stalk was still visible, however, cutting through the clouds as it spiraled out of sight overhead.

"How far up does this thing go?" the dragon wondered aloud. As strong a flier as Elridge was, the near-vertical flight was starting to take its toll. The dragon's sides heaved, his breath becoming ragged and uneven.

"Elridge, are you okay?"

"I...think...so," panted the dragon. "But...don't know...if...I can go...much farther. I've...never been...this high...before." He squinted into the clouds above. "Think...I see...something..."

Ivy strained to focus her eyes. Not far above, the stalk finally ended in a magnificent spray of emerald leaves. But there was something else—a streak of dark color. As they drew closer, Ivy was amazed to realize it was stone—a rocky ledge jutting out into the air alongside the beanstalk. Heavy vines clung to its rocky crevices.

"There aren't any mountains around here," she said, exceedingly puzzled. "Not even the Craggies are this high." The Craggies were a vast mountain range bordering the eastern edge of the kingdom. Ivy and Elridge had flown up and down its desolate, rocky slopes more than once on their adventures.

"Don't...care," wheezed the winded dragon. "Have...to set down...and...catch...my breath."

As Elridge skirted the beanstalk to come in for a landing, the tip of his tail brushed one of the heart-shaped leaves. Immediately, the nearest bean pod split open around the middle, revealing two rows of hooked teeth. The pod lunged at Elridge like a striking snake. With a strangled cry, the dragon barely managed to snatch his tail out of the way in time.

"Good goat fur!" he cried. He half landed, half stumbled onto the rocky ledge, his legs a tangle beneath him.

The dragon had set off an immense chain reaction. Down the length of the stalk, as far as Ivy could see, pods were jumping to life, baring their teeth and viciously nipping the air.

Elridge collapsed as far from the beanstalk as he could get. Lying on his belly, he struggled to catch his breath, his golden eyes the size of Cook's extra-large gooseberry tarts.

"I...knew...it," he gasped. "I...knew...there'd...be trouble."

It took several minutes for Elridge to catch his breath. Ivy used this time to take a quick look around, although climbing down from the dragon's back proved difficult in her tattered slippers. She ended up tumbling most of the way and landed on the ground in a heap of flowered skirts, her tiara of jasmine hanging over one ear. At least a carpet of lush green grass cushioned her fall a bit.

"I am *never* letting Drusilla pick out my clothes again," she growled under her breath.

There wasn't much to see, as clouds masked most of their surroundings, and there was no sign of Toadstool anywhere.

"Where could she be?" Ivy asked as the dragon gingerly rose to his feet.

"You don't think the beanstalk…ate her?" Even though there was no love lost between Elridge and the little goat, the thought still made the dragon pale.

Ivy glanced worriedly at the stalk. The pods were still snarling, whipping their sightless heads about in search of something to sink their teeth into. Toadstool had been nestled among the leaves at the top of the stalk, well away from the closest cluster of pods. Still, if she had slipped or tried to climb down…

Ivy shuddered. "Maybe she managed to jump to this ledge," she said, "and followed it wherever it goes."

"Ivy, look at this!" Elridge was examining the ground under his feet. He had been lying on top of two narrow ruts cutting through the thick grass.

"Those look like cart tracks." Ivy was incredulous. "Elridge, somebody's up here!"

The dragon's eyes darted about nervously. "Maybe we should go."

"We can't leave without Toadstool!" Ivy crossed her arms and fixed the dragon with an accusing stare. "What if she's in trouble? What if someone took her in that cart? Drusilla would never forgive us if we just abandoned her."

Elridge wilted under the princess's burning gaze. "Oh, all right," he relented, drooping his head in defeat. "But I'm doing this for Drusy, not for that annoying little fur-face."

Ivy suppressed a smile and quickly grew somber again. "Guess we're following these cart tracks, then. It's the only way Toadstool could have gone."

By this time, the frenzy at the beanstalk had died down. The pods had shut their snapping jaws and hung limply, once again looking like harmless green husks. Even so, Ivy was not sorry to start in the direction of the mysterious tracks, leaving the stalk and its collection of toothsome terrors behind.

The princess and the dragon trudged along at a pace a snail would have considered sluggish. Because of the thick clouds, it was hard to see more than a few steps in front of them. Ivy feared walking off another ledge and plummeting to the world below. When she voiced her concerns to the dragon, he suggested that she ride on his back.

"I've got us covered if we fall," he said, jerking his head back to indicate his wings.

"That might not be necessary," said Ivy, glancing around, surprised. "It looks like the clouds are thinning." For the past several minutes, the grassy ground had been sloping upward beneath their feet. The sun was getting brighter, the wisps of cloud now only as thick as a light morning mist.

"You're right," said Elridge, looking both pleased and relieved. "Good thing, too. We almost walked straight into this humongous tree."

Ivy, too, could now make out the span of dark, grainy wood blocking their path. It was very tall and very wide.

"Sheesh, the plants around here must get really big, like our beanstalk." The dragon paused thoughtfully. "That's strange. The cart tracks go right up to the trunk."

"Um…that's not a tree trunk," said Ivy. "Not unless the trees up here have keyholes."

"A door?" Stunned, Elridge looked up. What appeared to be an ornate brass keyhole with a bell-shaped opening as long as Ivy's forearm was embedded in the wood high above their heads. His gaze swept from left to right, taking in what was becoming visible through the rapidly clearing mist. "Good goat fur," he gasped, his jaw dropping.

They were at the foot of an enormous castle the color of night.

6

The Black Castle

In her wildest dreams, Ivy would have never imagined a castle as gigantic as the one before her now. Each of the black stones shaping its walls was the size of a boulder. Even Elridge was dwarfed by the massive door looming overhead. The cart tracks they had followed disappeared through the dark crack at the bottom.

"If Toadstool was with that cart, then she's inside now." Ivy inclined her head toward the hulking structure, feeling terribly small and insignificant beside it. "Do you think we should knock?"

Elridge looked as if she had just suggested they pour sugar water over themselves and play catch with a beehive. "Don't you see the *size* of this place?" he asked, shocked. "Do you really want to come face-to-face with whoever lives here? He probably eats little things like us for breakfast."

"Well, how else are we supposed to find Toadstool?" asked the princess.

"We *sneak* in," said Elridge, as if this were the most obvious thing in the world. "We can fly in through a window." He nodded at the rows of arched openings on either side of the door. They were so big that wagons could have rolled through them. "Once we're inside, we find Toadstool, grab her, and get out of here—before anything large and unpleasant has the chance to spot us."

Ivy didn't like the idea of sneaking into somebody's home, but Elridge had a point. The black castle didn't exactly give a welcoming impression, and who knew how the owner would react to a puny princess and little dragon showing up unannounced on his doorstep.

Rather reluctantly, she clambered aboard Elridge's back, and the dragon set course for the closest window. They sailed over the broad windowsill and into a vast hallway that stretched as far as a hay field in either direction. Suits of armor as tall as ships' masts stood at attention against the walls, along with iron candelabras the size of trees.

"Which way?" asked Elridge, looking from one end of the hallway to the other. The ends were mirror images, with nothing to suggest that one direction was any more promising than the opposite.

Before Ivy could answer, a burst of sound sent Elridge diving for cover behind the nearest suit of armor. It took Ivy a moment to realize the sound was a pair of angry voices—but far enough away that she couldn't make out the words. Then the voices grew louder, and she was able to catch snatches of heated conversation... "told you this cockamamy idea"... "how was I to know she wouldn't"... "should have known better than to...."

The louder of the two voices belonged to a woman. It was very shrill and very angry. There was a series of what sounded like high-pitched squeaks, and then: "FOR THE LAST TIME, SHUT YOUR WHINY YAP BEFORE I TOSS YOU OFF THE CLOUD CLIFFS!" It was the woman's voice again, rolling down the hall, making the suits of armor rattle as if they were marionettes dancing on the ends of invisible strings.

Ivy felt a tremor run through Elridge's body. "I hate to say it," she whispered to the uneasy dragon, "but that 'whiny yap' probably belongs to Toadstool."

Elridge gulped. "That means we have to head toward all the shouting, doesn't it?"

Ivy nodded. "But be sure to stay out of sight. Just get us close enough to see if we can spot Toadstool."

"Don't worry," said the dragon, a rather dismal look on his face. "The owner of that voice is *not* someone I want to meet."

He glided down the hall, flapping as little as possible so as not to stir the air with noisy whooshes of his wings. At the end of the corridor was an enormous room with high-back chairs and a wooden table as tall as the stable roof back home. Elridge landed, taking refuge behind a massive carved chest next to the door. Peering around a corner, they could make out the room's occupants on the far side of the chamber.

The woman sat in a cushioned chair next to the fireplace, only *woman* was not the word for her. She was monstrously big, surely an ogre or giantess—easily four times larger than any person Ivy had ever seen. She looked exhausted. A faded blue blanket shrouded a rumpled nightdress with a strip of lace pulling away from the hem. Hair spilled from the black braid that hung limply over one shoulder, and dark circles the size of melon slices shadowed the skin beneath her eyes.

Looking downright miniature by comparison was a man standing next to a rickety old handcart—a normal-size handcart, not a giant one. Ivy recognized the tattered green robes he wore, as well as the ash-wood staff he held at arm's length in a desperate attempt to keep its branches from wrapping him in a choking embrace.

"It's Gizzle the Green," she whispered. "I knew it! I knew that seedy plant mage was up to no good."

"And he has Toadstool," Elridge whispered bleakly.

Ivy had been so distracted by the sight of Gizzle that she hadn't paid much attention to his cart. Now she could see it was a very strange cart, indeed. For one thing, it had no handles. And instead of wooden slats, its sides were made of thick, woody vines, much like the ones she had seen climbing up the ledge where Elridge had landed. The vines kept writhing and wiggling in Gizzle's direction. An enormous bell-shaped birdcage took up the entire bed of the cart. Inside was not an oversize bird but a shivering, frightened-looking Toadstool.

"You promised me that foul fairy!" the giantess shouted at Gizzle. Her face was white with anger, making the shadows beneath her eyes even darker and more sinister. "You promised! Yet what did you drag back from the top of the cloud cliffs? Not that cursed Drusilla, but this whiny, worthless blot of fur!"

"The goat was the only thing at the top of the stalk," Gizzle replied. "Drusilla must have taken off the necklace I gave her." He sniffed contemptuously. "Probably wasn't good enough for her. Nothing I did ever was." His tone was bitter, and his knuckles tightened around his staff.

"Oh, why did I listen to you? Why did I let you get my hopes up?" The giantess's face crumpled, and she covered her eyes with her shovel-size hands. "I knew it was no use. I'll never get the harp back, not ever."

Gizzle looked rather sorry for her. "I've been trying to tell you for the past ten minutes," he said, with more patience than Ivy would have expected from the testy plant mage, "the goat whined and wailed the whole way here. Kept saying she was Drusilla's 'darling' and 'little treasure,' so I'd better let her go. If you had bothered to listen to any of her bellyaching, she'd have told you the same."

"Is that true?" The woman lifted her head and turned her bloodshot eyes on the goat with new interest. "Is Drusilla your mistress?"

"Y-y-yes." Toadstool's voice was even more high-pitched than usual. She was trembling so intensely that Ivy was amazed that she could speak at all. "And y-y-you had b-b-best let me g-g-go at once. There isn't anything Drusy w-w-wouldn't do for m-m-me, and s-s-she'll be terribly angry when she f-f-finds out you h-h-have me here."

Gizzle snorted. "What's she going to do? Use her froufrou fairy magic to turn us into tea cozies?"

But the giantess considered Toadstool's words carefully. "Nothing Drusilla wouldn't do for you, huh? Well, Gizzle, it would seem this pathetic creature might have her uses after all." The giantess rose from her chair and plucked the birdcage from the cart, hanging it high on a hook by the fireplace. Toadstool squealed as the cage rocked back and forth precariously.

"If this sniveling runt is really as precious to Drusilla as she claims, then Drusilla would do anything—give anything—to get her back," said the giantess, settling back into her chair, a touch of triumph on her sallow face. "We must make plans, Gizzle, but for the moment, leave me be. I'm tired and need to rest." Wrapping the blanket tighter around herself and laying her head against the back of the chair, she closed her exhausted eyes.

"Fine," said Gizzle, who looked a bit worn himself. "I need to prune my staff again, anyway. Blasted stick grows like a watered weed." He turned and shuffled toward the door with some difficulty, as the branches of his staff grasped at him desperately.

The vines on the cart seemed quite distressed by his departure. They shot out long, woody tendrils that pushed off the stone floor, propelling the creaky cart after him like a puppy trailing its master.

Elridge gasped and ducked back behind the chest as Gizzle hobbled in their direction. Ivy had a moment of panic as the plant mage passed their hiding place. There was a rustle like wind through tall grass as the flowers on her dress came alive, petals straining for Gizzle, tiny faces tracking his movement as sunflowers follow the sun. The honeysuckle vine at her waist started to grow again, finding its way to the floor and creeping across the flagstones like an octopus tentacle, making straight for the grubby plant mage. Ivy gripped it firmly in both hands and reeled it back.

Fortunately, the creaking of Gizzle's cart was enough to drown out the rustling of her gown. He was a good fifteen paces down the hall before the flowers on her dress stilled again.

"Well, that was interesting," Elridge remarked dryly.

"It has something to do with his green magic," whispered Ivy, once again finding herself wrapping an excess of honeysuckle sash around her waist. "Plants like him."

"Obviously," said the dragon.

They peeked out from behind the chest once more. The giantess appeared to have fallen asleep in her chair. Her eyes were still closed, her breathing, deep and rhythmic. Toadstool cowered in the birdcage by the fireplace, only an arm's length away.

"That latch doesn't look hard to open," said Ivy, eyeing the door to the cage. "We just have to be quiet so we don't wake her."

"We're not the ones you have to worry about making a racket," Elridge said sourly.

Ivy shared his concern. The easily excited Toadstool wasn't very good at keeping her mouth shut, even in situations that called for it most.

The little goat's head shot up when she spotted the pair of them gliding toward the golden cage, and Ivy pressed a finger to her lips to warn her to be silent. But by the time Elridge reached the finely wrought bars, Toadstool couldn't help but share some of her most pressing thoughts. "What took you so long?" she hissed indignantly. "Do you have any idea what I've been through up here? Where's Drusy? Why'd she send you clowns instead of coming herself?"

"Shhhhhh." Ivy glanced fearfully at the slumbering giantess, but she must have been very tired indeed. She hadn't stirred so much as an eyelash.

The latch to the cage was nothing more than a simple hook through a ring, easy enough for Ivy to slide apart as the dragon hovered alongside. She opened the door very slowly, just wide enough for the pixie goat to slip through. Luckily, the door's hinges didn't make a sound. Ivy motioned Toadstool forward.

"I hate flying," grumbled the goat, but she toddled toward the princess and dragon nonetheless. Then she stopped in her tracks. Her face scrunched like a squashed tomato, and her tiny pink nose wrinkled.

Ivy recognized the telltale signs, and her stomach dropped to her knees.

"It's... that... stupid... dress." Toadstool looked as if she was making a colossal effort to hold back the sneeze building inside her. "Shouldn't... have... come... near... me."

Elridge panicked. "Control yourself. You'll wake the bellowing behemoth over here."

"That would be difficult," thundered a voice from above. Toadstool's eyes widened, and Ivy felt as if the blood had frozen in her veins. The princess, the dragon, and the pixie goat slowly craned their necks upward. To Ivy's horror, a pair of bloodshot eyes peered down from an enormous face so tight with anger that veins as thick as earthworms throbbed at each temple. Before Elridge could react, a large hand shot out and clamped around the princess's torso, snatching her from his back. The giantess slammed the birdcage door shut with the other. "Did you think I was asleep?" She glowered at Ivy, her lip curling back in a snarl. "That would be a fine trick, since I'm NEVER asleep!" she roared. "Thanks to that blasted fairy Drusilla, I haven't slept in nearly a thousand years!"

7

Largessa

Ivy could barely breathe in the giantess's bruising grip. Flowers on her dress were crushed and released their fragrant perfume into the air. But all Ivy could smell were the billows of hot breath that scorched her cheeks and stirred her hair, for the giantess held the princess just inches from her flaring nostrils, examining her catch with dangerously narrowing eyes.

"Let her go!" cried Elridge, who looked ready to charge in spite of the raw terror on his face. His nostrils were starting to smoke, and Ivy knew he was about to breathe fire.

But before the dragon could make a move, flagstones shattered as several young, green vines burst through the floor. They grew at an alarming rate, lengthening and thickening before the princess's very eyes. One stretched high into the air, coiling around Elridge's scaly ankle.

"Get off me!" The dragon kicked in a desperate attempt to throw off the clinging vine, but to no avail. The stubborn plant dragged him down. A second vine latched onto the struggling dragon, then a third, winding around his legs, wings, and middle, until Elridge was flat on the floor with an entire mass of vines pinning him to the ground and clamping his snout shut. The vines grew dense and woody, putting out sprays of leaves. As a last touch, dangling clusters of purple flowers blossomed all over the dragon's leaf-shrouded body. One hung delicately from the tip of his nose.

"Thought I heard a commotion in here," said Gizzle the Green, limping into the room, his staff raised over his head. The vines, Ivy realized, were his doing—green magic.

"Wisteria?" The giantess arched a black eyebrow as she beheld the purple flowers adorning Elridge.

"*Wisteria sinensis* is a very sturdy vine," Gizzle said defensively. "Do you think just anything can hold down a dragon?" He lowered his staff, which was now neatly trimmed, although new branches were already starting to sprout. His gaze fell upon Ivy clutched in the giantess's hand. "Wait—I know you. You're that *Hedera helix* girl—Drusilla's goddaughter!"

"What?" The giantess looked surprised, then pleased, a smile spreading across her sickly face. Somehow, this was nearly as scary as seeing her angry. "You belong to Drusilla, too? Oh, this just keeps getting better and better! I'm going to make that heinous harpy regret the day she ever plotted against me."

Ivy felt a surge of indignation on her godmother's behalf. "What's Drusilla ever done to you?"

"What's Drusilla ever done to me?" The giantess looked incredulous. Then her face twisted with fury. Her grip tightened until the princess feared that her bones would be crushed. "I'll tell you what that odious little fairy did to me: She unleashed a

44

vile thief upon this castle to get her hands on our most precious treasures, and murdered my husband when he got in the way of her greedy plans."

Ivy's mouth fell open. "Drusilla would *never* murder anyone!" She found it a great effort to talk with the giantess's hand encircling her like an iron band but forced the words out, anyway.

"Well, she might as well have," growled Largessa. "It's her fault my husband, Megas, went chasing that plundering peasant down the beanstalk in the first place."

A mixture of anger and hurt darkened Gizzle's face. "And to make matters worse, Drusilla used one of *my* creations to carry out her diabolical deeds," he said. "It was *my* magic beans, *my* giant beanstalk she gave to that thieving farm brat."

"What thieving farm brat?" asked Ivy, exasperated. Nothing this rambling pair said made the slightest bit of sense.

"It was a long time ago," said Gizzle. "I had cultivated a variety of giant beanstalk grown from magic beans. It was fast-growing to boot, practically popped up overnight. This was a brilliant achievement in plant magic, but of course, those half-wits at B.B.I.M.F. wouldn't recognize genius if it bit them on their backsides. 'Totally impractical,' they said. 'Who'd want a giant beanstalk in their garden? Its size would make creating a balanced garden composition impossible, and the pruning would be a killer.'" Gizzle's eyes hardened at the memory. "Fertilizer-for-brains, every one of them! They told me to abandon the project, but I secreted away some of the magic beans for safekeeping. Drusilla stole a handful. I only found out recently. She slipped them out of my private seed collection without saying a word."

"And that was just the start of her wicked thievery," snarled

Largessa. "My husband and I kept a number of priceless treasures here in our castle in the kingdom of Gigantica. We had always assumed they were safe in our lofty realm."

"But Drusilla gave my magic beans to a human boy," said Gizzle. "What was his name again? John or James or something...."

"Jack," said the giantess, nose scrunching as if she had just swallowed swamp water.

"Yes, that's right—Jack." Gizzle's jaw clenched. "As I was saying, Drusilla gave this Jack my magic beans so he could grow a beanstalk tall enough to reach Gigantica. She had Jack climb the beanstalk and wheedle his way into this castle, not once, but *three* times, and each time he stole a precious treasure from Largessa and her husband. The first time he took a bag of gold."

"Megas loved counting that gold," said Largessa. "He'd sit at the table for hours every evening, sorting it into little stacks. Then he'd sweep the entire lot back into the bag and sleep with it under his pillow. The next night, he'd count it all over again, just to make sure none had gone missing during the day."

"The second time, Jack made off with a hen that laid golden eggs," continued Gizzle.

"Each egg was heavier than a lump of lead," Largessa said proudly. "They were solid gold the entire way through."

"And the last time, he took a golden harp that played the most beautiful music known to man or magical creature—all on its own, with no one stroking its strings. But this time, when Jack fled the castle and climbed down the stalk, Megas gave chase. Jack had a head start, however, and reached the bottom first. He took an ax and chopped away, until the stalk toppled. Megas fell to his death, and Jack got away with the golden harp."

Largessa burst into tears, which showered upon the princess like enormous raindrops.

Ivy's heart went out in spite of herself. "I'm very sorry about your husband," she said softly.

"Oh, fie on my swine of a husband!" Largessa raged through her tears. "He was a foul, bad-tempered, lazy brute. Not a day went by that I didn't regret marrying him. All he did was sit on his rump, bellowing at me to bring him his dinner, or his gold to count, or his hen to lay, or his harp to play. Never raised a finger to help himself. He deserved what fate he met, as far as I'm concerned. But that harp..." Her eyes shone with more tears. "Oh, how I miss that harp!"

"Largessa has terrible insomnia," Gizzle explained, casting a sympathetic look at the weeping giantess. "The music of the magic harp is the only thing that puts her to sleep."

"Since Jack made off with the harp, I've tried everything I can think of," sobbed Largessa. "Chamomile tea, counting sheep, warm milk, lavender baths, sleep masks, bedtime stories. I've drunk sleeping draughts by the boatload, but nothing works. Nothing! I'm as sleepless as ever!"

"Largessa hasn't slept in nearly a thousand years," said Gizzle.

Ivy suddenly felt tremendously sorry for the miserable giantess. No wonder Largessa was in such a bad mood.

"All because Drusilla sent that vile boy up here to fetch Largessa's treasures for her," fumed Gizzle. "Well, seeing as my beanstalk was used to commit Drusilla's crimes, I thought the least I could do was get that golden harp back for Largessa," he declared. "So I cultivated a new variety of giant beanstalk, one that would carry Drusilla all the way to Gigantica—and we wouldn't let her go until she agreed to return the harp. And this time, I made sure no one could climb up after her. No, my new and improved *mean*stalk is utterly unclimbable—a guaranteed loss of limb to anyone who tries!"

He gave a bark of laughter, but his mood quickly sobered. "Of course, cultivating a stalk with teeth was a rather dangerous undertaking for someone plants find irresistible," he said, glancing regretfully at his torn robes and injured leg. "My test stalks got terribly upset whenever I tried to leave them." It dawned on Ivy that the crescent-shaped scar on Gizzle's leg was actually a bite. And having seen the vicious pods on his so-called meanstalk, she knew exactly how he'd gotten it.

"And I didn't count on Drusilla putting my magic-bean necklace on a goat instead of wearing it herself," Gizzle continued bleakly. His gaze fell upon the vine-encased Elridge. "Or on having a dragon around who could *fly* up the meanstalk. Somehow, things never quite work out the way I plan—"

"But none of that matters now," interrupted Largessa, a gleam in her black eyes. "The three of you are our prisoners, and Drusilla will *have* to hand over the harp to get you back." Her lips curved in a cold smile as her gaze shifted between the captive princess, dragon, and pixie goat. "Or else."

8

A Rocky Bargain

"I wish I had a bigger birdcage," Largessa said to Gizzle the Green, casting her dark gaze to the cage where Toadstool cowered. "It's going to be a tight squeeze with a goat *and* a goddaughter, especially with all those ridiculous flowers"—the giantess wrinkled her nose at Ivy's poufy dress—"but I think I can make the girl fit, if I shove hard enough."

Ivy's heart tightened inside her chest. "Look, I know my godmother, and she would never steal from you or plot to kill your husband," she said desperately. "All of this is a terrible mistake. Drusilla doesn't even own a magic harp."

"Well, she'd hardly keep it out in the open where everyone could see it, now would she?" snapped Largessa, sounding as if only a harebrain would think so. "She'd have it hidden somewhere safe: a sealed cave that can only be opened with a secret password or an underwater grotto that can only be reached at low tide or some other out-of-the-way place where fairies stash their ill-gotten gains."

"There are no ill-gotten gains! Please, if I could just talk to Drusilla, I'm sure I could straighten all this out," pleaded the princess.

The giantess narrowed her eyes until they were little more than dark slits. "Hah! Do you honestly think I'm fool enough to just let you leave? I'd never see hide nor hair of you again. I am *not* going another thousand years without sleep, not when I'm holding the key to dreamland in my hot little hand." She gave Ivy a ferocious grin. "Gizzle," she barked, "get word to Drusilla that if she wants to see her goddaughter, her whiny goat, or this fumbling dragon ever again, she'll hand over the harp immediately."

"Wait!" cried Ivy. "If Drusilla does have the harp hidden in some faraway place, she'd have to travel there to retrieve it for you."

"So?" Largessa sneered impatiently.

"So Drusilla isn't in any condition to do that," said Ivy. "She was so upset when Toadstool was carried away by the mean-stalk, her powers went berserk. She can't take two steps without something disastrous happening. There's no way she could take a journey and bring the harp back undamaged."

Toadstool stopped quivering long enough to look smug. "Told you I was Drusy's little treasure," she told the giantess in a snooty voice.

Largessa made a sound halfway between a laugh and a snort. "You expect me to believe that Drusilla has lost control of her magic?"

"Why do you think she sent us after Toadstool, instead of coming herself?"

"Drusilla has a history of sending human children into my castle to do her dirty work," Largessa said spitefully.

Gizzle's face was bleak behind his stringy hair. "Actually… Drusilla's magic does tend to run amok when she gets upset," he said in a small voice, shooting the giantess a nervous glance. "Once, I accidentally sat on her favorite magic mirror—her cheer mirror, the one that tells you how wonderful you are every time you look in it—and she had a case of the hiccups that nearly burned down my entire greenhouse."

There was a long moment of silence, during which Ivy could almost hear the blood rising to Largessa's face. "You mean, after all this time, and all our planning, and all the fussing about with magic beans, I'm still…still…" The giantess's voice faltered, then exploded. "I'M STILL NOT GOING TO GET MY HARP BACK FROM THAT TWO-BIT FLIBBERTIGIBBET OF A FAIRY?"

The princess winced as her ears rang painfully. With her free hand, Largessa swept a giant inkwell off a nearby table. It smashed to pieces on the floor, releasing a dark stain that bled across the stones. Then, with a crash as loud as a thunderclap, she overturned the chair by the fireplace. Any remaining smugness was wiped from Toadstool's face as the little goat returned to quivering at the bottom of the birdcage. Elridge was frozen with fright beneath the tangle of wisteria vines.

"THAT'S IT! I'LL SHOW THAT SORRY FAIRY! THE GIRL, THE GOAT, AND THE TRUSSED-UP DRAGON ARE ALL GOING OVER THE EDGE OF THE CLOUD

CLIFFS. LET'S SEE HOW DRUSILLA LIKES IT WHEN THEY LAND ON HER DOORSTEP—WITH A SPLAT!"

"Now, Largessa, calm yourself," said Gizzle, backing away from the raging giantess. For the first time, the scruffy plant mage was starting to look scared, too. "Let's not resort to anything drastic. Remember, Drusilla's the one at fault here. There's no need for anyone else to get hurt."

"I DON'T CARE WHO GETS HURT," Largessa roared. She waved her arms in a wild fury, making Ivy's head spin so badly the princess was tempted to shut her eyes. "I DON'T CARE ABOUT ANYTHING EXCEPT GETTING MY HARP BACK!"

"We'll get it for you!" Ivy cried desperately.

"What?" Stunned, the giantess held Ivy in front of her face and fixed the princess with a disbelieving stare. "What did you just say?"

"It's what I was trying to tell you before," said Ivy, wishing she could cradle her dizzy head in her hands. "Since Drusilla's magic isn't working, someone else will have to collect the harp. That someone needs to be able to travel to whatever far-off place she's hidden it in. And unless you're willing to wait weeks, even months, to get the harp back, it had better be a fast method of travel, like, say"—Ivy let her eyes drift meaningfully to the imprisoned Elridge—"dragon flight."

Largessa followed the princess's gaze, realization dawning on her haggard face. "You and this dragon? The two of you will retrieve the harp for me?" Hope tinged with doubt replaced the anger in her voice.

"Just let us go, and I promise we'll bring it back," said Ivy. The princess didn't believe for a moment that her godmother had stolen Largessa's harp. But as long as she and her friends could leave the black castle in one piece, they'd worry about that later.

Largessa looked torn. She studied the princess carefully, as if trying to decide whether she could trust the girl. Long moments passed as Ivy's heart pounded painfully against her ribs. Finally, the giantess spoke. "Fine," she said, nodding at Ivy and the dragon, "the two of you may go. *Just* the two of you."

Toadstool's tawny eyes went as wide as gold coins. "Y-y-you don't m-m-mean...."

"The goat stays here. You can have her back when you return with the harp." Largessa grinned at her own cleverness. "After all, I need some sort of assurance that you'll keep your end of the bargain. And if this pathetic fur ball really is Drusilla's 'little treasure,' then Drusilla isn't likely to abandon her now, is she?"

Toadstool's knees were wobbling like a loose wagon wheel. "Y-y-you c-c-can't leave me h-h-here," she implored Ivy.

"Oh, dear little goddaughter doesn't have much of a choice," sneered Largessa, turning her attention back to the princess. "You have a week to retrieve the harp and return it to me. Otherwise, I feed the goat to the meanstalk."

Toadstool let loose a pitiful wail. She rocked back and forth on her hooves, looking ready to faint.

"What's more, just in case the little fleabag isn't as precious to Drusilla as she claims, I'll give you another reason to return the harp." The giantess thrust Ivy toward a large window in the back wall of the chamber. "Do you see those mountains?" Largessa gestured outside. In the distance, jagged peaks rose like black spires from the clouds. "The stones used to build this castle came from there. I can easily get more—many more. In fact, if the harp isn't returned to me in time, I will haul cartloads of stones to the edge of the cloud cliffs and toss them over one by one. Giant rocks raining down on your puny kingdom would do quite a bit of damage, I'd imagine. Your castle, your villages, your *people*—all would be crushed." She laughed rather savagely, and Ivy wondered if the lack of sleep had made her go a little mad. Even Gizzle looked shocked at her brutishness.

Largessa's laughter died down, her eyes growing as hard as the black stones of which she spoke. "Gizzle—take the girl and the dragon back to the cloud cliffs. I trust they can find their own way down." Largessa bent and dumped Ivy on the ground, towering over the speechless princess. "Leave this castle at once, little human, and don't dare return without my harp. You have one week."

Home Empty-Handed

The wisteria encasing Elridge parted with a wave of Gizzle's staff, although the plant mage left a few woody vines wrapped around the dragon's middle, pinning his wings to his sides. "Just a precaution, dragon," he said nervously. "So you don't think about attacking or breathing fire. Any funny business and those vines will squeeze the life out of you. They're very protective of me, so I suggest you be on your best behavior."

Toadstool was so hysterical, even Elridge looked sorry to leave her behind. Ivy could hear the goat's cries long after Gizzle had ushered them from the room and down the cavernous hallway. The walk back to the meanstalk was unnervingly silent by comparison.

Gizzle paused at the top of the cloud cliffs, wisely staying as far from the meanstalk as possible. A look of sincere regret hung over his bruised face. "For what it's worth," he said, "I'm sorry about Largessa flying off the handle like that. I don't want giant rocks raining down on your kingdom any more than you do. That isn't what I planned. But then, things never quite work out the way I plan." He knocked a pebble with his staff, sending it skittering across the cliff top.

"I didn't even know about any of this Jack business until a few months ago," he confessed. "One of my favorite fertilizer formulas calls for crushed quartz from the Isle of Mist, so I traveled there to collect some. I bumped into some of Drusilla's old fairy friends, and they told me the whole story. Thought it was hilarious—you know how fairies are. Drusilla had made no secret of it, bragging shamelessly about giving my magic beans to that boy."

Gizzle's face fell. "That's when it all started to make sense— Drusilla calling off our engagement, saying I was more interested in my work than in her." His features hardened. "Now I know it was all just an excuse. She never cared about me. She was just using me to get her hands on those magic beans. Once she had what she wanted, she didn't think twice about breaking my heart and tossing me aside."

"That doesn't sound like Drusilla," Ivy said pointedly.

"Then maybe you don't know her as well as you think. She had me fooled, too."

The princess was about to argue further, but Gizzle continued his story. "I was horrified to hear Largessa's treasures had been stolen and her husband slain—with my magic beanstalk at the heart of the plot. I have a conscience, unlike some," he sniffed. "I rushed to Gigantica to beg Largessa's forgiveness."

"But how did you get up here?" asked Ivy. "You couldn't have climbed a meanstalk." The princess herself stood at least ten paces from the plant mage, raising her voice to talk to him.

Even at that distance, the flowers on her battered dress twitched in his direction, as did the honeysuckle sash at her waist. Gizzle's own staff was grasping at him once again, and the grass around his boots rustled noisily as it stretched out to touch him.

"My dear girl, a mage of my magical ability has no need to climb a stalk like some lowly peasant," he scoffed, looking offended. "Surely you have noticed how lush and green it is up here. It's not a difficult task for someone with my magic to summon a vine or two whenever I wish. They grow all along the borders and edges of Gigantica." He gestured to the tangle of vines spilling over the cloud cliffs. "They're always more than happy to lift me into their land high in the clouds.

"And when I arrived here, things were far worse than I imagined. Largessa was in a terrible state, miserable and sleepless all these centuries. I knew I had to do something to help her, so I concocted the plan to get her harp back.

"It took weeks before my attempts to crossbreed a giant beanstalk with the carnivorous *Dionaea muscipula* were finally successful, yielding the first magnificent meanstalk. Drusilla's friends had told me about her wedding. It seemed the perfect place to set my plan into action. Why should Drusilla get her happy ending after making Largessa and me suffer so? I knew a few drops of Frimley's Magical Fast-Grow Formula would ensure a new meanstalk would sprout within minutes of Drusilla's receiving the necklace. The necklace itself was imbued with a bit of my own green magic so the meanstalk would be drawn to the last one who'd worn it, carrying her off. Once Drusilla was our prisoner here in Gigantica, she would have no choice but to hand over the harp to win her freedom.

"I thought it was foolproof." Gizzle heaved a great sigh. "I didn't mean to put your entire kingdom in danger. I only wanted Largessa to get her harp back and to put Drusilla in her place. Fortunately, it's an easy situation to put to rights. Just find out where Drusilla's hidden the harp, bring it back to Gigantica, and your kingdom is saved."

His staff was once again the size of a small tree. He had to pry several branches from his body before raising it high. The remaining vines fell from Elridge, releasing the dragon's wings.

"I'll try to keep an eye on your goat friend, but you'd better hurry, *Hedera helix*," said Gizzle the Green, slapping away another grasping branch. "You only have a week."

"Drusilla is going to be beside herself when she finds out we didn't bring Toadstool back," said Ivy, as the clouds parted beneath them and her father's castle came into view. This time, Elridge was careful to keep clear of the meanstalk and its ferocious pods. Fortunately, the flight down was not nearly as strenuous as the flight up had been.

"Do you think Drusy really stole Largessa's harp?" asked the dragon, his scalloped wings slicing the air.

Ivy was shocked by the question. "Of course not! How could you even think such a thing?"

Elridge glanced back at her, looking very uncomfortable. "Ivy, you know I'm fond of Drusilla," he said hesitantly. "And she's your godmother, so I know how much she means to you, but...." His voice trailed off uncertainly.

"But what?" asked Ivy, affronted.

"Well, you have to admit, fairies *are* awfully flighty," he said reluctantly. "And they can be kind of selfish. It's in their nature. Dear me, it would be just like a fairy to take what she wants, without any consideration for others. And Drusilla isn't always as... well, responsible as she could be."

"Drusilla's responsible!" protested Ivy.

"She pulled you from your lessons to pick ribbon colors and watch fidget flies," pointed out Elridge.

"Just because she likes to enjoy herself doesn't make her a thief."

"And she did walk out on you when you were a baby."

"I can't believe you're going to hold that against her!" cried Ivy. "You know she only left because she felt guilty about my mother dying." Blood rushed to her cheeks with a hot surge of anger. "How can you possibly doubt her, after all she's done for me, all she's done for both of us?"

"I didn't mean to upset you," the dragon said softly. Indeed, he looked very sorry that he had brought up this subject in the first place. "And you know I'm grateful for all Drusy has done. All I'm saying is that she's made some bad choices in the past, and we should prepare ourselves for the possibility that this is one of them."

"And I'm telling you, Drusilla would *never* steal that harp," Ivy said stubbornly. "You'll see. When we get back to the castle, she can tell you herself."

"Perhaps," said Elridge, who looked grimmer than ever. "The problem is, we're actually better off if Drusilla *does* turn out to be a thief."

The princess opened her mouth to object, but Elridge had already faced forward again, focusing on the fast-approaching castle. "Think about it, Ivy," his voice carried to her on the wind streaming past her ears. "If Drusilla *didn't* take the harp, then how are we supposed to find it in time to save Toadstool and keep Her Hugeness from crushing the kingdom with giant rocks?"

The stunned princess didn't have an answer.

Rose, Clarinda, Owen, and the king were waiting for them in the castle garden, gathered in a small group by the lily pond, well away from the foot of the meanstalk.

"Ivy, for goodness' sake, what took you so long? We've all been worried sick!" The king folded his daughter into his arms the moment she slid from Elridge's back.

Rose was so excited, she looked ready to burst. "Ivy, the pods—they're alive!" she exclaimed. "They have teeth!"

"Lots of teeth," Owen added, with far less enthusiasm. "We were all standing at the bottom of the stalk when the pods split open and started snapping." He held up his hand, and Ivy could see a long scratch on the back of his hand. "If I'd been any slower, I'd be missing a few fingers."

"I bet that was when I brushed against the top of the stalk," said Elridge. "One of those ferocious flytraps nearly took off my tail." He shuddered violently. "I can't believe the pods opened all the way down here. If you touch any part of the meanstalk, it must set off the entire thing! No wonder Gizzle said it's unclimbable."

"What is a meanstalk? And who is Gizzle?" The king held Ivy at arm's length, taking in her disheveled appearance. "Ivy, my dear, what's happened to you? Where's Toadstool?"

"Um, we ran into a little problem bringing her back," said the princess.

"Nothing 'little' about it," muttered Elridge. Ivy ignored him.

"Toadstool's okay, isn't she?" Clarinda's doe eyes were bright with worry.

"For now," said Ivy. "But I need to talk to Drusilla immediately." For the first time, Ivy realized her godmother was nowhere in sight. "Where is she?"

"Well, we couldn't just let her stand around in the garden," said the king. "Her magic was turning the place into a madhouse. So Boggs took her to her bedchamber for a rest. We hoped it might help with her hiccups."

"I need to see her right away—and Father, you need to come, too. It's very important."

Ivy noticed that the aftereffects of Drusilla's magic were visible throughout the garden. The frilly red frogs were sunning themselves on lily pads in the pond, and a small crowd had gathered around the mermaid topiary, who was singing her heart out to their utmost delight. The white butterflies had apparently found their way back to the garden as well and were fluttering around some sweet peas twining up a trellis. They made a beeline for the princess as soon as they spotted her, causing her to dash into the castle ahead of her father and friends. She wasn't about to let them take up fluttering around her dress again.

She met Tildy in the hallway outside Drusilla's second-story bedchamber. The nursemaid wrapped her thick arms around the princess. Ivy wished she could have stayed in the warm, lavender-scented embrace for a while.

When they broke apart, Tildy gaped at the state of the princess's gown. The butterflies were missing, the flowers around the middle had been flattened and crushed, and there were unsightly gaps where petals had fallen or blown away. Even the honeysuckle sash drooped rather pathetically, perhaps missing Gizzle and his enticing green magic. "Oh, Princess Ivory. Can't you ever wear anything nice without ruining it or ripping it to shreds?"

"Sorry," lied Ivy, who wasn't the least bit remorseful about the dreadful bridesmaid dress. "I need to speak to Drusilla immediately. How is she?"

"Better, for the moment," said Tildy, who looked exhausted. Strands of hair had escaped their pins and hung untidily around her face. "But those hiccups have been a royal pain. I brought Drusilla a soothing cup of tea, and she turned it into a snapping turtle. Then she set her bed sheets on fire. Fortunately, she found an old bottle of magic elixir in the back of her wardrobe—Hippolyta's Hiccup Helper. She's been much better since taking it. Who knows how long until the effect wears off, however, so if you want an uninterrupted conversation, I suggest you talk fast."

10

The Fairy's Tale

Drusilla was lying in her canopied bed, still in her sparkling white wedding gown, propped up by half a dozen pillows that surrounded her like lacy clouds. Boggs sat in a chair next to the bed, holding her hand. Drusilla might not be hiccupping uncontrollably anymore, but she was not happy.

"What's taking them so long?" fretted the fairy. Her eyes were rimmed in red, and her skin had paled to the color of the cream that Cook skimmed off the top of the milk jugs in the castle kitchen. "They should have been back by now. Oh, what if something's gone wrong? What if they couldn't find Toadstool? I'll never forgive myself if anything's happened to her."

"There, there." Boggs patted his wife's hand reassuringly. "Everything will be fine, love, you'll see."

The princess hastened into the room, followed by her father and friends, who had caught up with her outside the bedchamber door. Tildy swept in as well. Relief washed across Drusilla's beautiful features as she caught sight of them. She sat up eagerly, violet eyes as bright as burning stars. "Ivy, you're back! I knew you'd save Toadstool! Oh, look at your beautiful bridesmaid dress." The fairy stared sadly at Ivy's ruined gown. "But I suppose as long as Toadstool's all right, nothing else matters." Drusilla's gaze traveled past the princess, lingering in the doorway expectantly. "Where is she? I want to wrap my arms around my fuzzy-wuzzy Toady-Woady and never, ever let go!"

Ivy's heart plummeted. Drusilla would be inconsolable once she learned Toadstool was being held prisoner by an angry giantess in a black castle in the sky.

"Toadstool's fine," she said gently, sitting on the edge of Drusilla's bed—no easy task given the size of her skirts. They puffed up around her, pulling away from her feet and exposing the nearly shredded lady slipper orchids serving as shoes. "She'll be coming home soon, I promise."

The expression on Drusilla's face froze. "Soon? She isn't with you?"

Ivy's throat had gone uncomfortably dry. "I'll explain everything, but first I need you to tell me about Largessa and a boy named Jack."

Elridge's face appeared outside the large bedchamber window. The dragon was holding himself in place by clinging to the ledge with his front claws. Despite her ill humor toward him, Ivy was glad he was there. She wanted him to hear the truth from Drusilla's own lips.

"Largessa? Jack?" Drusilla's brow furrowed as if she was struggling to grasp a memory fluttering, like a pesky moth, just beyond reach. Not for the first time, Ivy found herself wishing that fairies were not quite so absentminded.

"Gizzle the Green is under the impression that you gave Jack some magic beans to grow a giant beanstalk," prompted the princess, "and that you had Jack climb the stalk to steal treasures from a giant named Megas and giantess named Largessa. And that Jack killed Megas when Megas tried to climb down the beanstalk in pursuit."

A stunned silence settled over the room.

"Well, I never," the king said indignantly. "What a despicable accusation to make! How could anyone think Drusilla would be involved in such a plot?"

A swell of satisfaction rose in Ivy's chest, and she had to resist the urge to shoot Elridge a triumphant look. No one else doubted her godmother.

The only one who didn't look grievously offended was Drusilla herself. "Oh," she said in a shrunken voice. "*That* Largessa; *that* Jack. My, that was a long time ago, back before I even became a fairy godmother. I had almost completely forgotten."

Ivy blinked. "You don't mean... you didn't really send Jack up a giant beanstalk to steal treasures and kill a giant"—her voice cracked sharply—"did you?"

"No—no, of course not," Drusilla said quickly, but she seemed reluctant to look Ivy in the eye. "Although in a way, everything that happened *was* my fault. You see, I did give Jack those magic beans." Her voice was heavy with regret. "I suppose I should have known it wasn't a good idea. He always was a bit of a bad seed, but I didn't realize what he was truly capable of. You have to believe me, Ivy. I didn't know any of those horrible things would happen."

The princess swallowed. "So why *did* you give Jack the magic beans?"

Drusilla lowered her head. "I was trying to help his poor mother. She had a lovely little farm, not far from the edge of the Fringed Forest, where the barley meadows are today. This was nearly a thousand years ago, not long after I'd left the fairy realm for life in the mortal world, back before there was a castle here in Ardendale, or even a kingdom called Ardendale at all." Her eyes softened with memory. "I wandered the world in those days, on one of those flying horses from the Isle of Mist." Ivy recalled the beautiful flying horses she had seen on her brief visit to the fairy kingdom. "Everything—every hill, mountain, and meadow, every raindrop clinging to a fern frond or wild violet purpling the forest floor—was so new and exciting, so very different from the colorless crystal of the fairy realm. I wanted to see it all! And this beautiful valley was always one of my favorite places to visit. That's part of the reason I took the post of fairy godmother to the royal princesses of Ardendale in later years, while other fairies sought appointments with the larger, fancyshmancy kingdoms of the North. Quaint and small as it was, I truly loved it here!

"Every time I visited the valley, I used to look in on Jack's mother, secretly. Humans were still very new to me, and I had never seen anyone so selfless and kind before. Fairies, as you know, aren't like that at all. But she was always setting out seeds for the robins and squirrels, and saucers of milk for the cat who had taken up residence in the hayloft. I think she even sensed my friendly presence. I used to find little sweet cakes left outside the cottage window."

Drusilla's violet eyes dimmed to a muted lilac. "Sadly, this poor woman's life took a turn for the worse after her husband died of fever. Suddenly, she had to manage the farm all by herself—no small task for one meager human. She did have a son, Jack, but her kindness had gone rather astray with him. He had grown up so spoiled and spoon-fed that he never did a lick of work, not even to help his own mother." Drusilla sniffed contemptuously. "After a while, the farm was in such bad shape that they had nothing to eat and no money to buy food. I couldn't bear to see Jack's good mother suffer, and I certainly couldn't let her starve. Then I saw my chance to help.

"Out of desperation, Jack's mother ordered him to take their last cow to the market and sell her for as many coins as he could get. By this point, I had met Gizzle on the North Continent, and we had become engaged, not that he ever had any time for me. He was always shut away in his greenhouse, fussing over his precious plants." Drusilla's voice turned sour. "He had just developed this ridiculous giant beanstalk, and I knew it was the answer to all of the farm's problems. With a beanstalk that big, they'd have an endless supply of food. Beans are terribly nutritious, you know, and just one giant bean is an entire meal. And they could sell what they didn't eat. Can you imagine what people would pay for something as unique as giant beans? Jack and his mother wouldn't hurt for money for the rest of their lives.

"Gizzle always got so crabby when I interrupted his work, so I just took a few of his magic beans one day while he was working on a new variety of magical marigold. I was sure he wouldn't begrudge a starving widow and her son a mere handful. I rushed back to this valley as fast as my flying horse could carry me. Those with powerful magic can convince mortal eyes that they're seeing something other than what's really there. With my meager abilities, I've never been able to pull off such a spell for more than a few minutes, but that's all it took. As I said, I was still very shy of humans, so on that day, I gave myself the guise of a friendly old man. I thought it would be hard to convince Jack to trade a cow for magic beans, but, fortunately, that boy always was as thick as a brick. He was more than happy to take them. His mother was very distressed, however. She flung the beans out the window, and the next morning, there was a giant beanstalk stretching to the sky."

A look of annoyance crossed Drusilla's beautiful face. "Now, a normal person who hadn't had a decent meal in weeks would think, 'Wonderful—a giant beanstalk covered in delicious beans,' not, 'Oh look, a giant beanstalk. I think I'll climb it and see where it goes.' But, like I said, Jack wasn't the brightest berry on the bush. Climb it he did, and he stumbled upon Megas and Largessa's castle in the clouds. You know the rest. It was a terrible tragedy, Megas falling to his death here on the valley floor, and all because I gave Jack those confounded beans."

"But surely you tried to return the stolen treasures to Largessa," said Ivy.

"Well...no," said Drusilla, shifting uneasily on her pillows. "You know how flighty fairies can be, Ivy. There were so many other things on my mind. I had to find a new home for the cow Jack had traded me. It's not like I could take her with me on my travels. I had to tell Gizzle that I had changed my mind about marrying him. And Jack's mother was no longer in danger of starving, since her son had given her a hefty pile of gold. So after the beanstalk was chopped down, I just sort of...forgot the whole terrible ordeal."

"You...forgot?" For a moment, Ivy was speechless, then words flowed forth in a heated rush. "But Largessa has been through so much because you gave Jack those beans. She can't sleep without the music of the golden harp that he stole. She's been miserable for a thousand years. The least you could have done was try to help her."

"I h-had no idea," stuttered Drusilla.

"Well, you never thought to check on her, did you? Not even after her treasures were taken and her husband killed."

Drusilla hung her head, ashamed. Grim disappointment descended upon Ivy like a winter chill. Drusilla might not have plotted the theft of Largessa's treasures or the murder of her husband, but she *had* left the giantess to suffer all these centuries without so much as a second thought. Elridge had been right: It was exactly the sort of selfish thing a fairy would do. There was a long, heavy silence before the princess could bring herself to speak again.

"What happened to Jack and the treasures he stole?" she asked, rather dreading the answer.

"Jack had big plans once he was rich," said Drusilla, her eyes turned downward, her voice so low it was little more than a whisper. "He thought a great destiny awaited him in the world beyond this little valley. So he left, taking his fortune with him."

11

Rescue Plan

Ivy cast her gaze to the flagstone floor. "The thing is," she said to her godmother, "Largessa wants her harp back, and seeing as she's gone so long without sleep, she's a little...bad-tempered. She's the one responsible for the meanstalk in the castle garden—well, she and Gizzle the Green. If we don't return the harp to Largessa within a week, she's going to feed...that is...well...Toadstool won't be coming back." As disappointed as she was in her godmother, Ivy wasn't cruel enough to spell out the dreadful details of Largessa's plan to feed Toadstool to the meanstalk. As it was, Drusilla promptly burst into tears. She grabbed a fistful of bed sheets and buried her face in the white folds.

"I'm afraid it gets worse," Elridge said from the window. Out of the corner of her eye, Ivy could see his dark scales glinting in the late afternoon sun, but she couldn't bring herself to look at the dragon, either. She suddenly felt very sorry for getting angry at him. "Largessa said she'll rain giant boulders down on the valley," said Elridge. "The kingdom will be crushed."

The lines on the king's face deepened, urgency etched into every crease. "Drusilla, you must have some idea where this harp is now."

Drusilla's shoulders wracked in sobs. "Ja-Ja-Jackopia," she choked out between tears.

"Jackopia?" The king's eyebrows arched. "This Jack, the one who climbed the beanstalk, is the same Jack who founded the kingdom of Jackopia?"

Drusilla could only nod mutely.

"Jack founded a kingdom?" Ivy was stunned. The awful Jack had been in charge of an entire realm?

"Jackopia is a very wealthy kingdom," said her father. "It's an island, actually, south of our shores, across the Speckled Sea."

"Which you would have known if you'd attended your geography lesson like you were supposed to," Tildy muttered under her breath.

"It's wh-where Jack w-went when he l-left Ardendale," blubbered Drusilla. "He s-sailed to an island far off the c-coast, b-built his own c-castle, and declared h-himself king."

"Rumor has it there's so much gold in Jackopia, it's a miracle the island doesn't sink under the weight," remarked the king. "The royal family is said to be a tad on the hoity-toity side, but I suppose people with such monumental wealth would get rather bloated heads."

"If the h-harp is anywhere, it's w-with them," said Drusilla, who was slowly pulling herself together. She took a deep breath and blotted her eyes with the sleeve of her wedding gown.

"I must speak with the king of Jackopia immediately." Ivy's

father straightened his spine, a determined look on his weathered face. "I am sure if I make a royal appeal, king to king, he will see to it that the harp is returned to its rightful owner. No doubt he is unaware of the unscrupulous manner by which Jack acquired it and will be eager to right the wrong committed by his ancestor. Perhaps I could impose upon Elridge for a ride across the Speckled Sea." The king's eyes drifted hopefully to the dragon in the window.

"Of course," Elridge said kindly. "I'm the Dragon Liaison to Ardendale, after all. I'll do anything I can to help."

"Your Majesty, if I might make a suggestion," said Boggs, who was still sitting at the bedside, clutching Drusilla's hand. "It might be best to have a contingency plan, just in case we're unable to get the harp back."

"What are you saying? Of course we'll get the harp back," cried Drusilla, sounding slightly panicked. "Toadstool is counting on us!"

"Of course we will, my love," said Boggs, squeezing her hand affectionately. "But on the tiny, itsy-bitsy off-chance that something does go wrong, we should plan to evacuate the kingdom *before* the giant rocks start raining down."

"A wise suggestion, indeed," said the king, stroking his beard thoughtfully. "Have the King's Guard make the necessary arrangements and gather the food, supplies, and wagons we will need to make it through the Fringed Forest to the North, if it comes to that. Gather the people to help. They will need to be alerted and assembled."

"With all due respect, Your Majesty, you're the best person for that job," Boggs said sagely. "At a time like this, the populace will look to their king for leadership."

"He's right," Ivy told her father, raising her head at last. "You stay here and help the kingdom prepare for Largessa's attack. I can take your request to the king of Jackopia as a representative of the royal family of Ardendale."

A look of concern crossed the king's face. "Ivy, it is a long way to go on your own."

"I'll have Elridge," said the princess, finally gathering the courage to turn her gaze to the dragon. She worried that he would be upset with her, but to her surprise, the look on his scaly face mirrored her own feelings of contrition. He gave her a tentative smile from across the room, and she smiled back.

"And me," Owen added firmly. "I'm coming with you. It's a straight flight across the sea this time, so no arguing that I'll slow you down."

Ivy was touched. She smiled at him shyly. "We'll be glad to have your company."

"I'm coming, too." Drusilla started to rise from her bed.

"You can't, love." Boggs laid a gentle hand on her shoulder to hold her in place. "Until you know Toadstool's safe, your hiccups could come back at any time. You have to keep taking your elixir."

"I can take the bottle with me," insisted Drusilla.

"There's not much left," said Boggs. "And it would hardly do for you to get stuck in a foreign kingdom, far from home, with another...disruptive...case of the hiccups."

"But I want to help!"

"I think Boggs is right, Drusilla," Ivy said solemnly. "You should stay here. After all, it was your 'help' that started this whole mess in the first place."

Drusilla looked as if she had been struck. "Oh," she said,

quietly. "I...I suppose I'll just stay here, then." She collapsed back against her pillows. Fumbling, she pulled a small hand mirror from her sleeve. Somehow, Drusilla always seemed to have an endless supply of little mirrors about her person. She held it out to Ivy. "You remember this, don't you?"

Ivy took the beautiful gilded mirror in her hands. It was framed by delicate golden rosebuds, the handle a flourish of carved vines. "It's the mirror that has a connection to all other mirrors, so you can talk to the people on the other side." The princess had used it once before, to contact Rose and Clarinda when she had been far from the castle.

"Take it with you," Drusilla said softly. Now she was the one staring at the flagstones. "Keep in touch, so we don't worry." She swallowed heavily, as if something was stuck in her throat. "And good luck."

Ivy felt a stab of guilt. Perhaps she shouldn't have been so harsh, and yet, she had only spoken the truth.

"Thanks," was all she could bring herself to say.

"Well," said the king awkwardly, "the three of you had best be going. Time is of the essence. Take the compass in the castle library and use it to fly due south, across the sea. You should reach Jackopia by morning."

There were quick hugs from her father and friends—and Tildy, who mumbled something about the princess doing absolutely anything to get out of her lessons. Drusilla sat silently on her bed. Ivy gave a quick good-bye nod in her godmother's direction. Then she and Owen rushed into the hall.

"I'll get the compass," said Owen, "and some bread and cheese from the kitchen. That'll have to do for dinner tonight."

Ivy wished she had snatched a slice of wedding cake when she'd had the chance.

"I'll meet you in the castle garden in five minutes," she told Owen.

"Where are you going?" protested the stable boy. "We're in a hurry, remember?"

The princess glanced at the battered gown clinging to her scrawny form. "I don't care how much of a hurry we're in. I'm not setting foot outside the castle until I get out of this blasted bridesmaid dress!"

PART TWO

Jackopia

12

An Eventful Arrival

"Ivy, Owen—wake up!"

The words seemed oddly distant, so the princess figured she must have imagined them. Beneath her cheek, her pillow was inexplicably stiff. Cool air was whipping past her face, stirring her hair. *This is a strange dream,* she thought. Then, *wait a minute—I know that voice.*

"I see the island! I see Jackopia!" said Elridge.

Jackopia. There was a stir of recognition in the back of her mind, and she eased open her eyes. It took a moment to realize that she wasn't in her bed at all. In fact, she was in a sitting position, leaning forward, and the "pillow" propping her head was actually a bony width of dragon spine. Ivy pushed herself upright and felt a tug of resistance. Glancing down, she saw a length of thick rope knotting her waist firmly to the spine.

Now I remember. Owen had had the forethought to bring rope to secure themselves, so that they could doze on the dragon's back without worrying about falling off. Ivy felt a warm rush of admiration for the stable boy; she was glad he had come along.

They had flown straight through the night, although Elridge had set down and floated on the surface of the sea a few times, to rest his wings. These weren't the most relaxing of breaks, however, seeing as the Speckled Sea had rather choppy waters. By the time they took to the air again, all of them were always covered in sea spray.

Now, the sky was awash in early light, but an equal glow radiated from below.

"Good goat fur, it's gorgeous. I've never seen so much gold in my entire life!"

Still a bit fuzzy with sleep, Ivy leaned to one side to take in the world below. Her breath caught in her throat, and she was instantly awake.

Beneath them, a massive mountain rose from the sea in a nearly perfect cone shape. Strangely, the mountain had no crest, only a gaping opening at the top. Ivy could see that the inside was as hollow as a rotted tree stump. Nestled on the floor of this enormous crater was a magnificent city covered in gold. Practically every surface shone with it—the cobbled streets, the rooftops, the sparkling fountains in the city squares, even the buildings themselves. At the very center, a spiraling castle was ringed by a moat with a solid gold drawbridge. Strangely, the walls of the buildings were dappled, as if made up of thousands of little dots.

"Wow, the whole kingdom's shinier than a new horseshoe," exclaimed Owen, greatly impressed.

Ivy was finding she had to narrow her eyes against the glare.

"Head for the castle, Elridge," she called to the dragon. "There's no time to spare." As urgently as Ivy needed to speak to the king of Jackopia, she also wanted to get Elridge out of the air. Dragons needed less sleep than humans. A dragon could stay awake all night in a pinch, but the princess knew Elridge needed to rest very soon. She was also determined to have a quiet moment with him at the first possible chance, so she could apologize for getting angry the afternoon before.

Elridge banked to one side and began his descent toward the gleaming castle. As he slipped within the bowl of the mountain, they were struck by a blast of heat so intense that Ivy's eyes first went dry, then started to water vigorously. Almost immediately, tiny beads of sweat welled on her forehead and along her hairline.

"Ugh, why's it so warm in here?" Owen asked.

"I don't know," said Ivy. "But look—that lake's got steam rising off it!" A small silver lake simmered on the outskirts of the city.

"I think it feels great," Elridge said with a sigh of contentment. Ivy was not surprised. Dragons were creatures of fire and enjoyed warm places. Elridge's own small clan lived among the red rises of the sandstone desert along Ardendale's western edge.

As they drew closer to the castle, people began to appear on the streets of the city below: peddlers pushing their carts, merchants making their way to their shops, housewives drawing well water for the morning washing. Even the carts and buckets on this island were made of gold, which, unfortunately, made them extraordinarily heavy. City folk were pushing and pulling with no small effort. Then, from far below, a shout of alarm reached Ivy's ears, quickly followed by others. Suddenly, people were diving for cover behind market stalls or scrambling to reach the safety of their homes. Others were pointing toward the sky, and frantic cries of, "Dragon! Dragon!" tore through the air.

"Oh no, I'd forgotten," said Ivy, raising a hand to her sweaty forehead. "People here aren't used to seeing dragons. Elridge, you'd better land—quickly!"

Elridge flapped madly for the castle. As they drew closer, Ivy could see that the strange texture of its walls was due to the fact that they were made up of countless golden ovals, stacked one atop the other like oddly shaped bricks.

"Those look like golden eggs," she said, recalling the story of Largessa's treasures. "I don't believe it. All the buildings on this island are made out of golden eggs!"

Elridge was still flying furiously, looking as if he planned to set down on the golden drawbridge. But they had been spotted at the castle, as well. Gold-helmeted heads appeared over the parapets atop the castle gate, and a heavy portcullis of golden bars came crashing down over the entrance. From the other side came a pressing cry, "Raise the drawbridge!"

But this was easier said than done. With a chorus of grunts and groans so numerous that Ivy suspected a good twenty men were winding the winch, the massive drawbridge lifted off the ground—but only by the slightest hairbreadth.

"Come on, come on! Put your backs into it!"

There was another series of groans, and the drawbridge hoisted a few inches higher. At this rate, it would be fully raised by lunchtime.

It must weigh a ton, thought Ivy. *It is solid gold, after all.*

"Fly up to the wall," she called to the dragon. "I can talk to them, explain who we are."

As Elridge neared the top of the castle wall, a series of long, golden cylinders appeared over the parapets. Ivy realized they were looking at an entire battery of cannons, aimed directly at them. She heard the heart-stopping hiss of a dozen burning fuses.

"Elridge, get out of the way!" shouted Owen.

But the dragon didn't have time to react. In several successive bursts, the cannons fired.

Elridge cried out and dived desperately, but he needn't have bothered. Gold cannonballs were apparently too heavy to fly far. Each one dropped nearly straight down. Several struck the rising drawbridge with noisy thunks, the added weight too much for the men trying to raise it. The drawbridge crashed back to the ground, followed by bleak moans of dismay.

At the sight of a dragon flapping directly overhead, the guards manning the cannons fled, stumbling under the weight of gold armor that must have all but roasted them in the oppressive heat.

"Where are you going, cowards?" cried a man Ivy assumed was their captain. She recognized his voice as the one that had called for the drawbridge to be raised. The visor of his helmet was up, giving her a full view of a taut face with a wide forehead, eyebrows drawn into nearly a straight line, so light in color that they were barely there at all. He raised a hand and pointed an armored-encased finger at Elridge. "I don't care if I have to stop you myself, dragon!" he shouted. "You'll not lay waste to this castle on my watch!"

"No one wants to lay waste to your castle," called Ivy. "We're here as friends."

But the man ignored her completely. With some difficulty,

he wheeled around one of the cannons so it was pointing in their direction. He tried, unsuccessfully, to lift a gold cannonball, a task that under normal circumstances undoubtedly required at least two sets of brawny arms.

"We're from the kingdom of Ardendale!" Ivy tried again, raising her voice even louder. "We only want to speak with your king."

Elridge set down on the castle walk, which was just wide enough for him to fit if he folded his wings. It was a good thing he was a bit small for a dragon.

The man was struggling to stand, the cannonball cradled in his arms like a bundled baby. "I'll teach...oversize invaders...to attack...my castle."

"Look," said Ivy, growing rather exasperated, "if we had meant to attack, don't you think we'd have done it by now?"

A swipe of Elridge's tail was all it took to send the man sprawling on his back, the cannonball rolling uselessly away. He immediately tried to rise, but a restraining claw on his chest applied just enough pressure to keep him pinned to the ground.

Having undone the rope around her waist, the princess slid from the dragon's back, marched up to the trapped man, and stared down at him.

"Now that we have your undivided attention," she said, "this dragon is not here to hurt anyone. I am Her Royal Highness Ivory Isadora Imperia Irene, Crown Princess of the Kingdom of Ardendale, and it is imperative that I speak with your king immediately."

Elridge removed his claw, and the man sat up gingerly.

"Well," he sniffed, carefully examining the chest plate of his gold armor, as if afraid the dragon might have left a mark, "for pity's sake, why didn't you just say so?"

13

The Elusive King of the Eggy Isle

Despite Ivy's insistence that she speak to the king at once, she was apparently not the only person eager to see the ruler of Jackopia, and no one in the shining castle was inclined to give her special treatment simply because her kingdom was in danger of being destroyed.

"But it's a matter of utmost urgency," she insisted to the Royal Schedule Keeper, a thin-faced, fastidiously attired attendant stationed to one side of the paneled gold doors that led to the throne room. "My kingdom is in great peril, and we haven't much time."

"Yes, yes, so you keep saying." The Royal Schedule Keeper didn't bother to look up from the enormous appointment book into which he was entering tidy rows of script with a sharp-tipped quill. Ivy wasn't surprised to see that the ink was gold in color, undoubtedly mixed from actual gold dust. The buttons on the man's doublet were also gold, and a white ostrich feather plumed from the top of his black velvet cap. The desk he wrote at was constructed of golden eggs. "His Majesty is extraordinarily busy, and his day is quite full. All of these individuals have appointments." He gestured to the crowd of people gathered in the gold anteroom. "As you arrived unexpectedly, you will have to wait for an opening to become available in His Majesty's schedule. Perhaps later today, or tomorrow..." He waved a dismissive hand, as if shooing away a pesky fly.

"I didn't realize I had to make an appointment to plead for the lives of everyone in Ardendale," snapped Ivy. She stomped back to a bench beneath a row of wide windows, barely able to contain her temper. She had been waiting all morning and hadn't been offered so much as a crust of bread. Her stomach rumbled in protest. It didn't help that the bench, which was also made of golden eggs, was hard, lumpy, and tremendously uncomfortable. The castle was stiflingly warm, just like the rest of the kingdom. She didn't know how the people bustling about in velvet overskirts and heavy doublets could stand it. Many were weighed down with loops of gold chain to boot.

Elridge and Owen had been forced to wait outside. Elridge, of course, couldn't fit inside the magnificent castle, and the waspish Captain of the Guard had refused to let the dragon rest in one of the numerous courtyards.

"Let a fire-breathing beast lounge within our castle walls?" he had asked incredulously, stiffening the set of his jaw. "Oh no, it's simply not possible. It would be an inexcusable breach of security. Plus, it would give the ladies of the court a terrible fright. The queen and her daughters are exceptionally delicate and sensitive creatures." He eyed Ivy, standing before him with tangled hair and a wind-rumpled gown encrusted with sea salt, as if to say, "*Unlike some.*"

"Elridge is perfectly civilized," retorted Ivy, who had to stifle her own urge to add, "*Unlike some.*"

"Be that as it may, I must insist that he remain outside," said the Captain of the Guard. "There is a stretch of meadow beyond the city, alongside the lake. Your dragon may rest there, provided he refrains from frightening the populace . . . again."

Ivy opened her mouth to protest, but Elridge cut her off.

"S'okay, Ivy," said the dragon, hiding a gaping yawn behind one of his claws. "Bedding down in a toasty meadow sounds lovely right about now."

"But it might not be safe." Ivy thought of the fearful residents of the city. As far as they knew, Elridge could still be a threat. What if one of them got it into his head to attempt to capture or even slay the dragon while he slept?

"I can stay with him," offered Owen. "Make sure no one comes near."

"That would be most appropriate," said the Captain of the Guard, with a haughty air. "The only servants allowed in the king's presence are his own royal staff."

And so Ivy had ended up on her own inside the glorious golden castle. The princess would have never imagined that there was so much gold in the entire world, let alone on one small island in the middle of the Speckled Sea. The floors were long, smooth stretches of gold, while the walls and furniture were dimpled with countless gleaming golden eggs. Even the everyday objects were made of gold—the frames of paintings, the tapestry rods, the tall vases spilling over with gold-dipped roses. Ivy, at first, was in awe of her lavish surroundings—until waiting hours in the stuffy heat outside the throne room ruined her mood.

During that time, she saw a number of individuals enter and exit to see the king. First were several men wearing large leather aprons. Next was a capable-looking man in a blue tunic embroidered with white feathers. Finally, over a dozen men with serious expressions, bearing stacks of parchment and leather-bound ledgers. They stayed inside much longer than the others.

Ivy slumped listlessly on her bench until she heard the delicate ding of a crystal chime. The double doors of the throne room were heaved slightly open by a pair of gold-armored guards. The immensely heavy doors were never opened fully; rather they were cracked just wide enough for one person to pass through at a time. The men she had seen earlier exited in an orderly line, making their way out of the anteroom. The Royal Schedule Keeper laid down his quill and rose to his gold-tasseled feet.

"What's going on?" asked Ivy.

"It's lunchtime," said the Royal Schedule Keeper. "The king is retiring to his personal chamber for his midday meal. And don't get any ideas about speaking to him on his way out. His Majesty has a private exit from the throne room. His meeting will recommence later this afternoon."

"You mean all those men are coming back?" Ivy moaned. "How long can one meeting possibly take?"

"I'm afraid you have picked a most inconvenient day to seek an unscheduled audience with the king," complained the Royal Schedule Keeper, yet again. "As I have said, His Majesty is incredibly busy. This morning he had appointments with the Master Goldsmiths and the Keeper of the Hens, and now he is meeting with his royal egg-countants."

"His royal accountants?"

"That's what I said—his royal egg-countants. A man of His Majesty's considerable wealth must attend to it closely. Egg-counting meetings have a tendency to run long.

"I'm off to eat my own lunch," said the Royal Schedule Keeper, meticulously placing a golden stopper into the inkwell on his desk. "Come back this afternoon. *If* the king has a spare moment, he may agree to see you." He shut the appointment book before him with an insolent little sniff. "But I make no guarantees."

Ivy marched past the gate guards, across the golden drawbridge, and along the shining streets that meandered from the castle, her boots pounding against the golden pavement. She ignored the curious stares of city dwellers and passersby, continuing until the buildings thinned, then gave way to open air, the road beneath her feet replaced by dry, dusty soil. The meadow of which the Captain of the Guard had spoken was more brown than green. The heat of the island was not particularly favorable to foliage, and it was especially sweltering here, next to the steaming lake. She was so angry that she had made short work of the lengthy walk.

Elridge rested comfortably on his side, his eyes closed and his long neck stretched out into the strawlike grass. Owen sat cross-legged on a blanket, sweaty but enjoying a roast turkey leg. He glanced up, looking both surprised and pleased to see her. "Ivy, where have you been? What did the king have to say?"

"I wouldn't know." Ivy threw herself down on the blanket next to him. "I haven't spoken to him."

"What?" Elridge cracked open an eye. "But you've been gone all morning."

"I know." The princess gritted her teeth. "He's been too busy with goldsmiths and accountants to see me. Perhaps this afternoon—'*if* the king has a spare moment, but I make no guarantees,'" she said, mimicking the snippy tones of the Royal Schedule Keeper.

"But Ardendale," said the dragon, sitting up in alarm, his serenity shattered. "The harp, the giant rocks—"

"No one seems to care," Ivy said with frustration. "All anyone at that castle does is ignore me or treat me like a royal nuisance." For the first time, the princess noticed that the blanket upon which she sat was covered with delicious offerings—a plate of turkey legs, a slab of bread, and a handful of ripe apples. "Where did all this food come from?" she exclaimed.

"Well, the rest of the castle staff might be snooty, but the scullery workers seem perfectly nice," Owen said cheerfully. "Word's gotten out that there's a dragon on the island—a friendly dragon. They came down to have a look. I didn't let them get too close, since Elridge was asleep, but they were impressed by the sight of him. None of them had ever seen a dragon before." The stable boy shrugged his shoulders. "They brought me lunch and everything." He gestured toward the assortment of food. "Would you like something?"

Ivy was already crunching hungrily on an apple.

"It's awful in there," she said between bites. "My father would never ignore a visitor to his castle, no matter how busy he was."

"That's it!" Owen snapped his fingers. "Can't you talk to your father in Drusilla's mirror? He's dealt with foreign royalty before. He'll know what to do."

"I suppose." Ivy set down her half-eaten apple and reached

into the top of her boot, where she had tucked Drusilla's gilded hand mirror. "But I don't know where he'd be this time of day. I have to give the mirror a location, somewhere there's another mirror."

"How about the one in Drusy's bedchamber?" suggested Elridge. "You know she'll be there. Boggs will make her stay in bed until there's absolutely no chance her hiccups will return. She'll know where your father is."

"I shouldn't bother her," said Ivy, trying to mask her reluctance to speak to her godmother. "Not when she's been feeling so poorly."

"It's the fastest way," insisted Owen.

Ivy sighed heavily, knowing her friends were right. Holding the mirror up to her eyes, she said, "I'd like to see Drusilla's bedchamber in the castle in the kingdom of Ardendale."

At once, the surface of the mirror rippled, as if it were a lake into which a pebble had been cast. When the waves cleared, Ivy was no longer looking at a reflection of herself, but at a tidy bedchamber with a large window and a canopied bed hung about with gauzy drapes. Drusilla was sitting up against her pillows, having traded her wedding gown for a white nightdress. Boggs was there, too, carrying in a wooden tray laden with a steaming bowl of soup.

"Drusilla, Boggs," Ivy called out to them.

Drusilla spotted the princess in the oval of glass above her wash basin. "Ivy!"

The fairy was out of bed in a flash, positioning herself before the gilt-framed mirror. "I'm so glad to see you! What did the king of Jackopia say? Has he given you the harp?"

"Actually...I've run into a little problem," Ivy confessed hesitantly. "I need to speak to my father. Do you know where he is?"

"He just finished consulting with his councillors about this giant-rocks-raining-down-on-the-kingdom business," said Boggs, abandoning his tray on Drusilla's nightstand. "I passed him in the hall on my way here. I'll just run and fetch him. He couldn't have gotten far." The spindly gatekeeper rushed out the bedchamber door, moving quite quickly for someone of his advanced age.

Left alone with the princess, Drusilla seemed uncertain what to say. She lowered her violet eyes, studying her hands apprehensively. "Ivy, before you left, I didn't get a chance to...that is...I just wanted you to know how much I regret—"

But the fairy didn't get a chance to finish her fumbling words. The bedchamber door burst open, and the king hurried in, tailed by Boggs and Tildy.

"Ivy!" he rushed forward to join Drusilla at the mirror. "What is it? Boggs says you've run into trouble."

"The thing is," said Ivy, face flushed with embarrassment, "the king of Jackopia won't see me. I don't have an appointment, and his staff says I have to wait for an opening in his schedule."

"But that's preposterous!" exclaimed Tildy, coming up behind the king. Ivy noticed that the plump nursemaid scrupulously avoided acknowledging Drusilla in any way. "Our entire kingdom is at stake, and they're worried about some shoddy schedule."

The king frowned. "Some royal personages can be of a rather formal and difficult nature. What have you said to his staff?"

"That I needed to speak to their king immediately," said Ivy. "That our kingdom is in danger and desperately needs his help."

"Oh Ivy," said her father, shaking his head. "That's not the way to deal with a situation such as this. You must tell them that you insist upon speaking to the king under Article Eight, Section Twelve, of the third Prickly-Aldwin North Interkingdom Convention. It requires a reigning monarch to hear the formal requests of a representative of another kingdom. The king will have to see you right away."

Ivy blinked. "Article Eight, Section Twelve?"

"Princess Ivory, you should have known that," scolded Tildy. "You told me you read the Prickly-Aldwin North Interkingdom Conventions."

"Well, I skimmed...part...of them," Ivy offered lamely, thinking back to the afternoon she had sneaked away with Drusilla and Elridge to watch fidget flies. Her nursemaid clicked her tongue, a look of fierce disapproval darkening her face. Drusilla turned away guiltily.

"Ivy, go now," urged the king, his expression solemn, his voice unusually grave. "You understand what's at stake here. It is vital we get that harp—no matter what."

14

Jack the Brave, Mighty, and Truly Magnificent

The words *Article Eight, Section Twelve, of the third Prickly-Aldwin North Interkingdom Convention* worked like magic, although the Royal Schedule Keeper looked less than happy about it.

"This will completely throw off His Majesty's schedule," he said with an unmistakable note of accusation. "Now his afternoon appointments will have to be completely rearranged, canceled even." He studied the heavily inscribed appointment book with distinct dismay. "But I suppose I must take your request to the king." He rose from his desk and signaled the guards, who cracked open the enormous double doors to the throne room so that he could slip inside. It was several minutes before he returned, casting a curt, "Very well, His Majesty will see you now," and yet another dismissive wave in Ivy's direction.

As it appeared the Royal Schedule Keeper had no further words for her, the princess turned and made her way to the golden doors. The guards heaved them open ever so slightly, and Ivy squeezed through the gap, emerging on the other side into the most beautiful room that she had ever seen. The floor was an inlay of white and yellow gold in the pattern of diamonds and stars. Massive gold chandeliers hung from the ceiling, candles cradled within golden eggshell halves instead of candleholders. The golden eggs forming the walls had been carved with elaborate reliefs of foliage and flowers. Paintings hung in even intervals around the room. Each appeared to depict the same man—a swaggering youth with coppery brown hair and a self-assured expression. He was engaged in a number of heroic acts: fearlessly scaling a colossal beanstalk; fiercely battling a ferocious giant with a sword; and triumphantly hefting a bag of gold, a snow-white hen, and a golden harp high into the air. Ivy had a sinking feeling she knew who the youth was supposed to be—not to mention the giant.

A raised dais at the far end of the room supported a series of golden thrones, flanked by servants wielding large feathered fans to cool the occupants. The largest throne bore a blue cushion, upon which sat an enormous man with a silver moustache. With his rotund body, an alarming lack of neck, and a girth that was widest around the middle, he looked a bit like an egg himself. He was covered in so much gold that Ivy didn't know how he managed to move. There was enough gold chain draped over his chest to haul up a ship's anchor. Each of his thick fingers sported a nugget-size ring, and his crown was as large as a fruit bowl.

"Well, don't just dawdle in the doorway," he said impatiently. "Now that you've interrupted my affairs, the least you can do is come in and tell me what it is you want."

Ivy hadn't realized she'd been lingering at the edge of the room, drinking in the spectacle of her surroundings. She hurried forward under the watchful gaze of the gold-clad guards standing at attention along the walls.

At her approach, the king of Jackopia narrowed his eyes, giving her a scrutinizing look. "So, you're the Crown Princess of Ardendale, are you?"

"Yes, Ivy—that is, Princess Ivory Isadora Imperia Irene." Ivy belatedly remembered that one was supposed to curtsy upon being presented to a royal personage. She swept one leg behind the other and dipped into a bow, but it was done so ungracefully that she wobbled and nearly fell over. The conspicuous sound of a half-suppressed giggle floated down from the dais.

The king's lips set in a grim line, as if he didn't approve of what he was seeing. He made a brisk gesture toward the throne on his left. "My wife, Queen Hortensia."

Queen Hortensia was very thin and looked faint. She fanned herself with a lace handkerchief. Gold chains draped off her bony form in a way that reminded Ivy of storybook sea hags dripping with seaweed. She took delicate sips from the golden goblet clutched in her hand. She acknowledged Ivy with the slightest nod of her head, as if she couldn't possibly make any greater effort than that.

"Our daughters, the Royal Princesses." The king indicated two pretty girls sitting on the opposite side of the queen. They were both about Ivy's age, although one was slightly taller, obviously the elder of the two. Gold bracelets encircled their wrists, gold drops fell from their ears, and tiny gold slippers encased their dainty feet. As if this were not enough, both girls had glorious cascades of golden curls. Ivy suspected the giggle had come from one of them. Even now, they regarded her with expressions that were half amused, half scornful.

"And our son, the Crown Prince." The king looked to his right, upon a boy many years younger than Ivy. The Crown Prince of Jackopia was surprisingly unimpressive. He was rather small to begin with, and the sizable throne upon which he sat made him seem all the smaller. Beneath hair that was the same coppery brown as that of the man in the paintings, brown eyes peered curiously. They were magnified by a pair of large round spectacles, giving him a slightly bug-eyed look. A solitary gold signet ring adorned his left hand.

"Is it true you flew to the island on the back of a fire-breathing dragon?" he asked, leaning forward excitedly.

"One-Oh-Three, that is hardly a suitable question," admonished the queen, looking scandalized. "We do not talk about fire-breathing beasts in this throne room. We certainly do not talk about such reckless and dangerous activities as flying on one. And sit up straight before you fall off that throne and hurt yourself." She took a long sip from the golden goblet.

"Yes, Mother." The boy straightened and dutifully fell silent, but not without a look of grave disappointment.

"My children often join me in the throne room with my wife and their tutor, Master Puckle," explained the king. For the first time, Ivy noticed a man standing stiffly to one side of the dais. He wore dark scholars' robes—and an even darker expression on his heavily lined face. "I believe it important to their education that they witness firsthand the running of a royal court." The king returned his haughty gaze to Ivy. "And what, may I ask, is so important that it demands my attention above all the other pressing matters to which I must attend?"

"My kingdom is in grave danger, Your Majesty," Ivy said solemnly, "and my father, the king of Ardendale, most earnestly requests your assistance."

The king of Jackopia didn't appear particularly moved by this. He sat fixedly on his throne, his face displaying all the emotion of a rock wall. "Go on," was all he said.

Ivy clasped her hands in front of her to keep from fidgeting nervously. "A long time ago, one of your ancestors, Jack, came to this island—"

Outraged gasps cut short the princess's words. Lifting her eyes to the dais, she saw the queen looking scandalized again and blood rising to the king's flabby cheeks.

"You must never, *ever* refer to the founder of our noble kingdom without using his full and proper title," said the king, affronted. "Jack the Brave, Mighty, and Truly Magnificent. It is one of our oldest laws, laid down by Jack the Brave, Mighty, and Truly Magnificent himself, to ensure that he always receives the respect he so richly deserves."

"Right. Sorry." Ivy cleared her throat uncomfortably. "A long time ago, Jack the Brave, Mighty, and Truly Magnificent came to this island and brought with him a golden harp."

"Yes, everyone knows the story of our celebrated ancestor." The king's countenance brightened, and he slipped into the easy rhythm of an often-told, much-admired story. "Long ago, when this isle appeared as no more than an unnamed speck on the edge of most maps—if it appeared at all—Jack the Brave, Mighty, and Truly Magnificent was a courageous young lad living in a beautiful valley on the mainland. The local populace would have had a happy existence, except a giant of most fearsome size and temperament terrorized the land. Every evening, after a day of raiding farms and villages, devouring livestock, and carrying off a human or eight for a midafternoon snack, the giant would retire to his castle in the clouds, only to return upon the morrow. The entire valley lived in mortal fear. But Jack the Brave, Mighty, and Truly Magnificent refused to stand by while his friends and neighbors fell victim to the giant's wrath.

"With not a single thought for his own safety, he fearlessly ascended a giant beanstalk—the only route in or out of the giant's realm—and confronted the monstrous brute directly. The giant was furious that a mere human dared to trespass upon his lands, and he set about trying to smash Jack the Brave, Mighty, and Truly Magnificent with an enormous club of stone. But Jack the Brave, Mighty, and Truly Magnificent was a quick and clever lad. He ducked and dodged every blow, darting here and there until the giant's head spun so badly that he dropped his weapon. As he bent to retrieve it, Jack the Brave, Mighty, and Truly Magnificent drew his father's sword—which he had had the foresight to carry with him—and loped off the giant's head in one fell swoop. He returned home a hero, and the people agreed that his brave deeds should be rewarded with the giant's treasures: a bag of gold, a hen that laid golden eggs, and a golden harp that needed no fingers to strum its strings. Jack the Brave, Mighty, and Truly Magnificent took these prizes, sailed to this isle, and established our glorious, gold-filled kingdom." Pride shone on the king's face, almost as brightly as the rings on his thick fingers.

"Um ... that's slightly different from the version I heard," Ivy said tentatively. She sensed she was going to have to be very careful with her words. The king seemed to think a great deal of Jack. "Largessa—the wife of the giant—claims that Jack the

Brave, Mighty, and Truly Magnificent...well, sneaked into their castle and stole the giant's treasures out from under his nose."

"Stole? Balderdash!" cried the king. "It was his courageous deeds that earned him those treasures." A fierce scowl twisted his lips. "Of course, I'd expect the wife of such a barbarian to lie about such things."

"The thing is, my fairy godmother, Drusilla, was there," said Ivy, "and she says Jack the Brave, Mighty, and Truly Magnificent really did steal those treasures."

"Absurd," snapped the king. "Outsiders have long been envious of the wealth and proud history of our magnificent kingdom. They make up all sorts of stories to discredit our founder."

"Well, whether or not Jack the Brave, Mighty, and Truly Magnificent stole the treasures really isn't important," said Ivy, deciding to try a different approach. "Largessa is demanding that the harp be returned to her. She's threatened to shower giant rocks upon Ardendale if it isn't back in her cloud kingdom within seven days—well, six now that we've flown all night to get here. That's why my father sent me to seek your help. We hoped the royal family of Jackopia still had the harp."

"Of course we still have the harp," said the king, a bit indignantly. "It's not like we had to sell it to afford the royal silverware—not that we'd ever resort to using something as second-rate as silver."

Ivy felt positively weak with relief. "Thank goodness!" she exclaimed. "Then Ardendale is saved! I can return the harp to Largessa."

The king gave an imperious sniff. "Absolutely not," he said.

"What?"

"The harp is a national treasure, one of the original

treasures that Jack the Brave, Mighty, and Truly Magnificent brought with him to this island. It is an important part of our kingdom's history."

"But Ardendale will be crushed!" cried Ivy.

"Perhaps you should consider sending someone to lop off the giantess's head," suggested the king. "It worked last time."

"It *is* only a harp, Father," ventured the young prince, blinking sympathetically behind his large spectacles. "We never even use it. It just stays locked away in the royal vault."

"That's because it's far too valuable not to be under lock and key," declared the king. "This is a good lesson for you, One-Oh-Three, one you must remember when you are king. Jackopia possesses treasures that other kingdoms can only dream of. We are the only kingdom that can boast a golden castle, a golden city, golden fountains, golden furniture, golden salad forks. And as soon as the royal shipbuilders find a way to make golden ships that don't sink to the bottom of the sea, we'll have those as well. Why, I'd cover the grass in gold, if I could. No other kingdom has golden grass, and how I love having golden marvels that no one else can claim." The king's eyes gleamed greedily. "Our unrivaled wealth is what makes Jackopia superior to all other kingdoms. Never part with more of your fortune than absolutely necessary, especially something as wondrous and rare as a golden harp."

Ivy's temper flared like a freshly lit torch. "I can't believe you think your fortune is more important than the lives of everyone in Ardendale," she burst. "That's the most selfish thing I've ever heard!"

The queen fanned her lace handkerchief furiously, looking lightheaded. "Well, I never," she said, taking a long draw from her golden goblet. "Such impertinence! How dare you take that tone of voice with His Majesty!"

"It is all right, Hortensia," said the king. "Decorum is obviously not something they teach princesses in Ardendale, nor could someone from such a meager kingdom possibly appreciate the importance of wealth as we can. Why, they have one of those castles made of stone." He glared down at the princess, hard and unfaltering. "I will overlook your outburst in deference to your royal title, but I bid you carry a message back to your father. The golden harp belongs to my royal family, as it has for hundreds and hundreds of years. There is absolutely no way, under any circumstance, that I will allow it to leave Jackopia. Not now, not ever."

15

Thick as Thieves

"Jack the Brave, Mighty, and Truly Magnificent? Good goat fur, someone sure thought a lot of himself." Elridge wrinkled his scaly snout in disgust.

It had been evening by the time Ivy had returned to the meadow, and she had been too tired and upset to tell her friends the details of all that had occurred before the king. The princess knew she could have probably begged a guest room at the castle, but she was still fuming and found she'd rather sleep in a field than spend the night under the same golden roof as the hard-hearted royal family of Jackopia. And so she had passed a restless night next to the steaming lake, uncomfortably warm even in the enveloping darkness. Owen had insisted she lie upon the blanket provided by the scullery workers, but it provided little in the way of comfort. She could feel the dry, scratchy meadow grass straight through the thin fabric. Morning found Ivy and Owen munching on what was left of the food from the castle—Elridge, after gorging himself at Drusilla's wedding banquet, wouldn't need to eat again for at least a week or two—and Ivy told her friends of her disastrous royal audience.

"And that's not the worst of it," she said. "Jack convinced everyone on this island that he was some sort of big hero. They think he got the harp by defeating Megas in battle and saving the countryside from the giant's evil rampages."

"And it sounds as if Jack's descendants have heads as big as he had." Owen lifted a cold gaze toward the golden towers of the castle, rising above the rooftops of the city. "Worrying about how much gold they have, how rich and important they look, when our kingdom is on the brink of destruction. Those muckety-mucks are as shallow as a muddy hoofprint." He turned away with disgust, as if the castle's soaring spires and magnificent archways held no appeal for him now.

Ivy sat dejectedly on a large rock in the middle of the meadow. "What am I going to do? I can't go back to Ardendale without the harp." She propped her chin in her hands and pressed her lips together in frustration. "Some future ruler I'm turning out to be. In five more days, there won't be a kingdom left to rule anymore."

"We'll think of something, Ivy, I promise," said Elridge, giving her an encouraging smile. "And for the record, I think you're going to be a great ruler. You just need a little practice is all."

Ivy tried to return the dragon's smile but couldn't muster more than a half-hearted twitch of her lips. "Thanks, Elridge." Once again, remorse settled over her, heavy as damp wool. "I never got the chance to tell you how sorry I am for getting angry at you. You were right about Drusilla all along."

"No, I wasn't," the dragon said sharply. "I'm the one who owes *you* an apology, Ivy. I shouldn't have thought the worst of Drusilla. She didn't take the harp."

"She might as well have," grumbled the princess. "Jack would never have had the chance to steal the harp if it wasn't for her, and Largessa wouldn't have been miserable all these centuries. It's no wonder she wants to destroy our kingdom. Drusilla should have done something to help her!"

"Well, Drusy didn't actually know Largessa wasn't sleeping all this time," pointed out Elridge.

"She knew Jack had killed Megas and stolen his treasures," countered Ivy. "She knew Largessa had suffered at Jack's hands. She didn't even care!"

"It's not that she didn't care," said the dragon. "She just didn't think about it. It's not exactly the same thing."

"Well, she *should* have thought about it. What normal person would forget something like that?"

"Ivy, that's just it. Drusilla's not a normal person," Elridge said with great shrewdness. "She's a *fairy*." A brooding look came over his long features. "I've been thinking about this a lot since we left Ardendale. I was being too hard on Drusilla, and I think you are, too. A fairy's natural instinct is to be selfish and thoughtless. Drusilla has to fight against that all the time. Sure, she can be flighty, but I think she's doing pretty well, all things considered. Remember what the fairies were like back on the Isle of Mist? They barely acknowledged our existence. But Drusilla has a conscience. She became a fairy godmother, didn't she? Whatever her faults, Drusy cares about people. She cared about your mother"—the dragon regarded the princess pointedly—"and she cares about you."

His scaly face softened. "This harp business happened a long time ago, Ivy, not long after Drusilla left the fairy realm. She's grown a lot since then, and she obviously feels terrible about what happened."

Ivy was once again struck with a stab of guilt. Perhaps Elridge was right. Perhaps she *had* been too hard on Drusilla.

"Look, it's that fussbudget captain from the castle!" said Owen. "What's he doing here? I hope this doesn't mean trouble."

Ivy raised her head and caught a glint of gold on the road from the castle. It was indeed the punctilious Captain of the Guard. He still wore his suit of golden armor, although he had removed his helmet and tucked it beneath one arm, revealing a blunt head shaved bald against the heat. His walk to the meadow must have been an extraordinarily strenuous one. No doubt the inside of his armor was as hot as hearthstone. By the time he reached the stretch of brown grass, his brow was dripping and he was panting from the effort. He didn't pause at the field's edge but marched straight to Ivy's rock, his armored feet leaving deep indentations in the dry soil.

"Imagine...a man...of my position...being reduced...to delivering messages," he huffed. It took several more gulps of air before he could speak normally. "This"—he thrust a neatly folded square of parchment at Ivy—"is for you." Without waiting for her to open it, he blurted, "It is a summons from His Royal Highness."

"A summons?" The princess unfolded the heavy parchment. Written in small but flawless gold script were the words:

Princess Ivory Isadora Imperia Irene is hereby summoned
by command of His Royal Highness, the Crown Prince of

Jackopia, and is to present herself at the castle with the most immediate of haste.

"I've been ordered to escort you to see the prince," said the Captain of the Guard. "So on your feet now. It's a long walk, and it wouldn't do to keep His Highness waiting." He took hold of her arm as if to tug her into a standing position.

Ivy was getting a little tired of being pushed around by the surly castle staff. "I need a moment with my friends," she said defiantly, more to be difficult than anything else. She jerked her arm from his grasp. "You interrupted us in the middle of an important conversation."

The Captain of the Guard sputtered indignantly. He looked as if he was about to argue. Then his eyes drifted to the long, gold-paved road back to the castle. His fire fizzled. "Fine, yes, whatever," he said wearily. "Just don't take too long. His Royal Highness is expecting you. I'll wait by the roadside." He strode back toward town and leaned heavily against the trunk of a scrubby olive tree next to the road, where he proceeded to mop his forehead with a gold-embroidered handkerchief. Ivy suspected he hadn't given in out of consideration for her. The captain looked like he could use a rest before trudging back to the castle in his cumbersome armor.

She snorted in disdain. "It's bad enough that the royal family of Jackopia refuses to help us. Now they think they can just snap their fingers, and I'll come running like some obedient servant."

Owen flushed at her words, and Ivy suddenly could have kicked herself for making that servant remark.

"You're not in trouble, are you?" the stable boy asked with concern.

"How can I be?" asked Ivy. "I haven't done anything...I don't think." She shrugged and grudgingly rose from her rock. "I guess I better go find out what this is all about."

"I wish I could come with you." Owen's face was a mixture of helplessness and regret, perhaps even a little shame.

Ivy wished he could come, too, but she remembered how the Captain of the Guard had dismissed him from the castle the morning before. The stable boy probably suspected, as she did, that any effort to join her now would meet with the same result.

"I'll be okay," she said, trying to reassure him. "I'm sure it's nothing serious." She turned to Elridge. "I really am sorry about getting upset." She was suddenly reluctant to leave until she knew the dragon had forgiven her. "We're okay, aren't we?"

"Of course," said Elridge, with an airy wave of his claw. "Right as rain. Close as clams. Thick as thieves."

Ivy had begun to stride in the direction of the road but found herself stopping and spinning in her tracks. "Elridge—that's it! You're a genius!" she whispered, the words brimming with excitement.

"What's *it*?" The dragon's forehead creased. "What is it? What did I say?"

"That's how we're going to get the harp back," said Ivy. "What this situation calls for is a little bit of thievery."

"Thievery?" Elridge's eyes widened in shock. "You want to steal the harp?"

Owen shot a nervous glance toward the road, but the fussy Captain of the Guard was still dabbing at his face with his handkerchief, gazing off in the direction of the city, where the streets were starting to fill with morning bustle. "Ivy, don't you think that's a little drastic?"

"Not at all," declared the princess. "We're running out of time, and my father said to get the harp back no matter what." She raised her eyes to the golden castle, a look of fierce determination hardening her face. "Besides, turnabout is fair play. If Jack can steal the harp, then we can steal it back."

16

One-Oh-Three

The princess could have reached the castle gate fairly quickly had she been by herself, but the gold-laden Captain of the Guard had to stop and rest three times as they made their way through the city. Each time, he laid his helmet on the ground and bent over to plant his hands on his knees, drawing deep, rasping inhalations.

"Just...catching...my...breath," he panted each time in way of explanation.

"Why didn't you just take off your armor before coming to get me?" Ivy asked with a touch of annoyance.

"As if...I'd ever...do something...so impertinent," wheezed the captain. "Our golden armor...is a symbol...of our king-dom's...great prosperity."

"You mean the king likes to show off how much gold he has," the princess muttered to herself. But in all truthfulness, she was no longer upset about having to return to the extravagant castle. Now that she had made up her mind to steal the harp, she needed to figure out exactly where the royal vault was located.

"Speaking of prosperity, the king must need a special place to store his massive amounts of gold," she said, making an effort to keep her tone casual.

"Mmmmm," said the Captain of the Guard. Apparently, he was too busy trying to breathe to make conversation.

Their prolonged journey didn't end once they reached the castle gate. After crossing the drawbridge and a spacious courtyard of cobbled gold, the Captain of the Guard led her down a long gallery where larger-than-life gold statues of Jack the Brave, Mighty, and Truly Magnificent gazed upon passersby. Then they turned down another hall, this one thankfully Jack-free, and traversed a second, smaller courtyard before climbing a spiral staircase to a circular, sunlit chamber. Another guard in golden armor flanked the doorway.

"The prince's private sitting chamber," said the captain, as if Ivy should be greatly impressed.

A lush blue rug covered the golden floor, and plump cushions adorned large chairs formed from golden eggs.

"Your Highness," said the captain to the diminutive, bespectacled boy perched atop one such chair, his lap barely large enough to contain the huge book he was poring over. "Princess Ivory Isadora Imperia Irene to see you, as you requested."

The crown prince of Jackopia lifted his head from the book, his studious expression melting into an eager smile.

"Oh excellent!" he exclaimed. "I've been waiting."

The Captain of the Guard gave a jerk of his head, which Ivy took as a signal that she should step forward. She eased into the room, wondering if proper etiquette dictated that she should curtsy to the small, mousy-looking boy. She suddenly wished she had finished the books on royal protocol that Tildy had given her. She was saved from this embarrassing dilemma when the young prince unexpectedly heaved aside his thick tome and hopped off his chair rather indecorously, rushing forward to greet her.

"I'm so glad you haven't left the island yet," he said. He moved his hands in excited gestures as he spoke, and Ivy was reminded of a puppy who couldn't keep still. "I was afraid you might have gone. But one of the servant girls was in the city very early to get pickle relish for Father's poached eggs—Father absolutely has a fit if there isn't pickle relish for his poached eggs, you know—and she's the same servant girl who brings my morning wash water, and she said you and your dragon were still in the meadow by the lake, because she had seen you as she walked by. Since I didn't get a chance to talk to you yesterday—and I really wanted to talk to you—I drew up a summons immediately. I've never drawn up a summons before. I hope I did it correctly. I copied most of the words from an old summons my father once sent, only I changed the names. I asked Brom to take it to you. Thank you for delivering the summons, Brom. You may leave now"—here, the prince paused long enough to give an airy wave in the direction of the Captain of the Guard—"and now here you are. I'm so very, very pleased. Tea?" He gestured to a solid gold teapot and set of golden teacups on a table. "I'm afraid it's not hot," he said apologetically. "Mother is afraid I'll burn myself, so I'm only allowed to drink it lukewarm."

"Um, no thank you," said Ivy, amazed that the prince seemed to have managed this considerable ramble without drawing a single breath.

"If you're sure there's nothing else, Your Highness," said the Captain of the Guard from the doorway.

"No, thank you, Brom," said the prince. The captain gave a stiff little bow, exited the chamber, and disappeared down the spiral staircase.

"I'm glad he's gone," confessed the prince in a whisper. He ushered Ivy to the far side of the room, out of earshot of the remaining guard, whose eyes, Ivy couldn't help noticing, followed them unwaveringly. "Don't get me wrong. I like Brom well enough. It's just that Mother would have a fit if she knew I had brought you here to ask this—and I didn't tell Brom that she didn't know—but what's it like?"

Ivy was puzzled. "What's what like?"

"Flying on a dragon, of course," said the prince. "I wish I could have gone down to the meadow to see the dragon myself. I was so jealous when I heard that some of the scullery workers went. Sometimes I wish I were just a common boy. Then I could leave the castle and do things like see a dragon. But I'm not a common boy, am I? And there's no way Mother would ever let me get within a hundred—no, two hundred—paces of a real-live, fire-breathing dragon in any case—"

"Wait a minute. You're not allowed to leave the castle?" Ivy's eyes widened in shock. "Ever?"

A look of resignation clouded the prince's face. "I've stayed inside the castle walls my entire life," he said sadly. "I've never been to the city or to the lake. I've never even crossed the drawbridge to the other side of the moat."

"That's awful," said Ivy, who couldn't imagine being trapped in one place her entire life. "Why won't they let you leave?"

The prince sighed forlornly. "I was very small when I was

born," he said. "Too small. I nearly died. The royal healers worked day and night to keep me alive, and I was sick for a very long time. Even though I got better, Mother still worries that something will happen to me. I'm still small for my age, you see, and Mother thinks it makes me frail. She keeps telling me that I can leave the castle when I get bigger and stronger; but the thing is, I don't think I'm ever going to get big, not as big as other boys, anyway. But Father says we must do our best not to distress her. She has terrible nerves."

"So they force you to stay inside the castle? All the time? That's ridiculous!" said Ivy.

"I'm surprised *your* father let you fly all the way to Jackopia on the back of a dragon," remarked the prince. "We had heard he made you his heir. My father says a girl shouldn't rule a kingdom. My sisters are only educated in noble matters so they will make suitable royal wives, although I don't see why a girl shouldn't be allowed on the throne. Doesn't your father worry that something will happen to you?"

"Of course he worries, but that doesn't mean he's going to lock me in the castle like a prisoner," Ivy said with obvious disdain.

There was an awkward silence, and she worried that she had been too blunt. The prince looked embarrassed, and Ivy wondered if she should apologize. But the moment passed quickly, and the burning curiosity returned to his eyes.

"Tell me about the dragon," he said. "I've only ever seen illustrations of them in books. He must be huge!"

"Well, Elridge is actually a little small himself, for a dragon, that is." Ivy was amused by his eager interest. She was finding that she liked the young prince. If not for his fine clothing and the gold signet ring on his finger, he could have been any number of young boys back home in Ardendale, the sons of villagers or the castle staff, all aflutter at the thought of a dragon nearby. "Don't get me wrong—he's plenty big. Sometimes we go on picnics on the other side of the kingdom. Elridge can carry me; my friends Owen, Rose, and Clarinda; and my fairy godmother and her husband." There was a slight catch in her voice at the mention of her fairy godmother. Ivy cleared her throat and forced herself to continue. "That's about his limit, though, and he flies slower when he's carrying so many people. When it's just me and him, Elridge can shoot through the sky like an arrow."

"Wow," said the prince, eyes bright behind his overly large spectacles. "Has he flown you many places?"

"Oh yes," said Ivy, enjoying the prince's rapt attention. "Over the Craggies, to the Smoke Sand Hills, through a swamp inhabited by these awful swamp sprites. We even went to a fairy kingdom once and fought off a lake monster. And don't get me started on the trolls—"

"Trolls?" The prince's mouth formed a wide, astonished "O." "Leaping lava, what I wouldn't give to see a troll...but Mother would have a fit. Hah! She would have a fit if I even *talked* about trolls. I can hear her now." He straightened primly and spoke in a pinched tone. "'Trolls are not a topic of polite conversation, One-Oh-Three. You shouldn't bring up such dangerous subjects, or you may overexcite yourself.'" Ivy was tickled to discover that he did a very good impression of the queen.

"Why do your parents call you One-Oh-Three?" she asked.

"It's my name," said the prince. "Well, actually, my name is His Royal Highness Prince Jack the One Hundred and Third, but my family calls me One-Oh-Three for short. You can call me One-Oh-Three, too, if you'd like," he added shyly.

"There've been one hundred and three Jacks?" Try as she might, Ivy couldn't keep the astonishment out of her voice.

"It's a law laid down by Jack the Brave, Mighty, and Truly Magnificent," the prince said sheepishly. "All of the kingdom's princes are named Jack, and all of the princesses Jacklyn. My sisters are Jacklyn the Ninety-Seventh and Jacklyn the Ninety-Eighth, but we call them Ninety-Seven and Ninety-Eight. Shortening our names like that is tradition, too. Some generations have a good number of princes and princesses, and it can get pretty confusing when you've all got the same name."

Ivy shook her head in amazement. Was there no end to Jack's enormous ego?

"Where did all these golden eggs come from?" she asked, gesturing to the egg-dappled walls. "Surely one hen couldn't have laid all the eggs in the kingdom?"

One-Oh-Three laughed. "Of course not," he said. "The eggs come from the Hen Hive."

"The Hen Hive?"

"Yes," said the prince. One corner of his mouth curled thoughtfully, and for a split second he seemed torn. Then his face cleared as if he had come to a decision. "I'm supposed to be studying," he said. "But I don't suppose any harm's done if I take a break, just for a few minutes." He seized the edge of Ivy's sleeve and tugged her toward the door, a look of excitement in his buggy eyes. "Come on! I'll show you."

17

Golden Eggs Galore

One-Oh-Three led Ivy on another twisting journey through the corridors of the golden castle. The princess was glad to have him as a guide. She could have never navigated the labyrinth of halls and passages, anterooms and archways on her own. The only thing she could be sure of was that they were headed down, into the lower levels of the castle. The prince had ushered her down two separate sweeping staircases. The guard from the prince's sitting room followed them at a short distance.

"I can't go anywhere without a guard," the prince told Ivy, his sour face making clear his feelings on the matter. "A guard even stands outside my bedchamber door at night. Mother worries I'll choke in my sleep."

It was very warm in the depths of the castle, the warmest place on the island yet. The halls they traveled now were windowless and sparsely decorated, lit only by the glow of torches along the walls. One-Oh-Three hurried Ivy down one last set of stairs, this one narrow and far less grand than any of the others. At the bottom, they passed two workers in tunics embroidered with white feathers, like the one worn by the man Ivy had seen entering the throne room. Beyond two enormous pillars were arched double doors. Unsurprisingly, the doors were solid gold, and once again they were flanked by a pair of guards in golden armor.

"That's the entrance to the Hen Hive," One-Oh-Three said proudly. "We keep the hens right here in the castle, so the guards can watch over them. They're the source of all the kingdom's gold. You can go inside if you'd like. I'm...not allowed." A little of the sparkle left his eyes. "Mother is afraid I'll have an allergic reaction to chicken feathers." He gave a wave at the guards, who heaved open the doors so that Ivy could pass.

She entered an enormous room alive with the clucking of hens. Stray white feathers floated down like fingers of snow, swept from the floor by another worker in a tunic, busy with a broom. It was easy to figure out why this part of the castle was called the Hen Hive. The lofty golden walls were domed like a beehive and covered from floor to ceiling with small niches stuffed with straw. Hundreds of white hens nestled comfortably within these. A long, thin groove spiraled along the walls, running beneath the niches. Ivy quickly discovered the groove's purpose. Every few seconds, a metallic clank echoed throughout the room, followed by a rattle like a noisy wagon wheel. Golden eggs were heavy, and unlike regular eggs, didn't break easily. Each time one was laid, its weight caused it to roll from its niche, which had a slightly slanted bottom to encourage this action. It fell into the groove and proceeded to spiral down the walls until it landed, with a clang, in a large golden wheelbarrow at the bottom. With so many hens, it was only a matter of minutes before the wheelbarrow was stacked with eggs. A worker in a feather tunic wheeled it away; another brought an empty one to take its place.

No wonder there are so many golden eggs in this kingdom, thought Ivy. *Those hens lay faster than Tildy doles out reading assignments.*

Curious, she followed the worker with the piled-high wheelbarrow, who slipped through a side door that she hadn't noticed before. Inside was a room with golden tables the length of small piers. Dozens of workers sat here, all wearing feather tunics and all doing something very strange. They appeared to be sorting eggs by the way each one sounded. Workers held eggs up to their ears and tapped them lightly with a tiny hammer. After evaluating the sound this created, they tossed the egg into one of the large crates on the floor or one of the golden baskets on the table.

"What are you listening for?" Ivy asked the closest worker, a round man with ruddy cheeks.

Luckily, he seemed as cheerful as his rosy coloring suggested. "Well, someone has to separate the soft gold from the hard gold, now, don't they?" he said pleasantly.

"Soft gold?" asked Ivy, puzzled.

"A yoke," explained the man. "Most of the eggs from the Hen Hive are solid gold, but some only have a golden shell. Inside is a yoke. You can tell which ones have yokes because they have a bit of a hollow ring to them." He held an egg to his ear with one hand and used the other to tap it with his hammer. He was rewarded with a heavy clank. "Solid," proclaimed the man, tossing the egg into a crate on the floor. He gestured to the eggs in the basket before him. "These have yokes. It's very important not to get them mixed up with the solids. If someone tried to use one of these to build a wall or a chair, it would start smelling something awful after a week or two. Nothing worse than the stench of rotten egg built right into your furniture." The man chuckled. "These will go to the hatcheries, if the Hive is in need of new chicks. Otherwise, it's off to the kitchens."

Ivy balked. "You can *eat* golden eggs?"

"Of course." The man looked amused. "Not many crops will grow in this toasty climate, but we have golden eggs aplenty. Takes a bit of work to crack open the shells, but the kitchen staff has an assortment of hammers and chisels that do the trick. The king swears the quality is superior to that of regular eggs. He refuses to eat anything else."

"What happens to the solid ones?" asked Ivy.

"The king's egg-counting staff takes charge of them. They keep track of all the king's gold, even the broken eggshells from the kitchens. They count every single egg and keep a very careful inventory. If eggs are needed for construction or furniture-making, an application must be made to egg-counting. If gold needs to be melted or molded, to make a candlestick or signet ring or toenail trimmer, for instance, egg-counting will send eggs to the forges. In the meantime, they're stored in the royal vault."

Ivy's ears pricked. "Is that nearby?"

The man gave her an inquisitive look, perhaps finding this a curious question.

"I mean…golden eggs are so heavy," she added quickly. "It would be a lot of work to move them very far."

A worker pushing a wheelbarrow heaped high with eggs chose that ill-timed moment to make an appearance.

"More for you, Bertrand," he said to the ruddy-cheeked man, gesturing to the pile.

The round man sighed and turned from Ivy. "Sorry, going to have to get back to work if I'm to finish this new batch by lunch."

The princess was sorry, too.

One-Oh-Three was waiting for Ivy when she exited the Hen Hive through the weighty double doors.

"So what did you think?" he asked eagerly, the golden sheen of the walls around them reflecting yellow in his spectacle lenses.

"It's pretty impressive," admitted Ivy. "Are all those hens descended from the one Jack the Brave, Mighty, and Truly Magnificent brought to the island?"

"Every single one," said One-Oh-Three. He sounded proud again, although a note of wistfulness had crept into his voice as well. "I wish I could have adventures like Jack the Brave, Mighty, and Truly Magnificent. He wasn't stuck inside the castle, drinking lukewarm tea. Just think of his amazing feats. He was one of the greatest rulers in history!"

"He was something else, all right," Ivy muttered.

"I'm really sorry Father won't give you the harp," said One-Oh-Three, as they started up the stairs. "I would, if I were king. I mean, just think of all the people in danger. How awful! And what will you do, now that your kingdom is going to be destroyed?"

"Um...I'm not really sure," said Ivy. She could hardly tell the prince that she planned to steal the harp before that could happen.

"I've been thinking," said One-Oh-Three, "that you should request sanctuary."

Ivy paused on the stairs in midstep. "Sanctuary?"

"You know, under the Waldgrave Act of Royal Protection," said One-Oh-Three. He began to recite a passage with such fluid ease, it was obvious he had memorized it long ago. " 'A reigning monarch shall not deny sanctuary to a person of royal blood in danger of bodily injury or harm should he or she return to their native kingdom.' " He peered down at her from the step above, his face as bright as a harvest moon. "Don't you see? Father can keep the harp from you, but he can't force you to return home. You could be crushed by falling rocks. If you ask, he'll have to provide you sanctuary here in the castle. It's the perfect solution. You'll be safe, and you can stay and tell me all about your adventures with your dragon friend."

It wasn't the perfect solution, of course, for all of One-Oh-Three's boyish optimism. Ivy was about to say that she could never remain in the safety of this beautiful castle while her father and friends were still in danger, but she caught herself, her mind suddenly awhirl with possibilities. There were still five days until Largessa's deadline. During that time, it would be very useful to have access to the castle to find the royal vault....

"Tell me all about this Waldgrave Act of Royal Protection," she said to One-Oh-Three, slipping a friendly arm around the prince's scrawny shoulders.

Tildy was right, she thought ruefully. *I really need to study more.*

18

Sanctuary

"**Y**ou said I'd do *what?*" Elridge squawked in a way that reminded Ivy uncannily of a chicken. Then again, after her visit to the Hen Hive, perhaps she just had chickens on the brain.

"It was the only way I could convince the king to let you stay," the princess said apologetically. She had spent most of the morning and afternoon at the castle before returning to her friends' encampment next to the steaming lake.

"B-but I don't know anything about being a guard dragon," sputtered Elridge, rustling his wings nervously. "I'm lousy at guarding things. You should know. Remember how I just flew off when I was supposed to be guarding you in the white tower?"

"Of course I remember," Ivy said impatiently. "I flew off with you. Come on, Elridge, how hard can it be? It's not like anyone in this kingdom actually wants to steal gold. They're surrounded by the stuff. Guarding it is all for show, to make the king feel rich and important."

Not an hour had passed since the princess, as One-Oh-Three predicted, had been granted sanctuary by the king of Jackopia. The young prince had dragged her back to the magnificent throne room, where he was to join his family and Master Puckle for another afternoon of royal observation. The king had looked none-too-pleased to see her again, and he all but burst the gold buttons on his doublet when she brought up the Waldgrave Act of Royal Protection.

Queen Hortensia and her daughters looked aghast.

The queen took several long pulls from her golden goblet before turning to the king. "Surely there must be some other kingdom that could take the girl in," she said, flapping her lace handkerchief as furiously as the wings of a startled bird.

"Why, now that I've seen this glorious island, nowhere else could possibly compare," Ivy said innocently, rather enjoying their discomfort. "As you've said, Jackopia is far superior to any other kingdom."

The king heaved a sigh so deep, the mass of gold chains rose and fell on his chest. "I am afraid my hands are tied, Hortensia," he said, shifting uneasily upon his blue cushion. "We cannot force the girl to return to her doomed kingdom. That is the law. If she wishes it, Princess Ivory must be permitted to stay."

The queen emptied the rest of her goblet in one large and very unladylike gulp.

"But that monstrous dragon must leave our shores at once," declared the king. His flabby face grew stony and resolute, and the princess suddenly felt far less smug. "Nothing in the

Waldgrave Act of Royal Protection says I have to let some savage beast despoil my golden isle. And the scaly brute can take that servant boy of yours right along with it. I have no obligation to protect some lowly peasant."

"But Owen is my personal page," said Ivy, thinking quickly. "Who will attend to me if you send him away? I suppose your kindhearted daughters wouldn't mind sharing their ladies-in-waiting with a fellow princess."

Ninety-Seven and Ninety-Eight looked as if they'd rather take a dip in the steaming lake. "Father!" protested Ninety-Seven.

"Oh, very well," grumbled the king. "Keep your servant then. But that oversized lizard has to go."

"That's too bad," said Ivy, again doing her best to sound innocent. "Just think of the opportunity you'll miss."

"What in melting magma are you talking about?" asked the king, exasperated.

"It seems to me that a king with a fortune like no other should have a guard like no other to keep it safe. Just think what the other kingdoms would say if they found out you had your very own guard dragon? They'd be positively green with envy."

"A guard dragon to watch over my precious gold?" The king's face lit with all the delight of a child being presented with a new toy. "Yes, that would be most fitting! I could have the royal goldsmiths forge a suit of golden dragon armor, the likes of which the world has never seen, and the beast could stand guard outside the royal vault, protecting my treasure from any who would dare lay a thieving hand upon it."

Ivy fought the urge to point out that dragon scales were

harder than iron and that Elridge hardly had need of a suit of armor. She knew the king got excited about anything that he could cover in gold.

"I'm sure Elridge would consider it a great privilege to serve the royal family of Jackopia," she said, bowing her head as if the king had just bestowed an immense honor.

Of course, Elridge considered it nothing of the sort, but after returning to her friends in the meadow next to the lake, the princess did her best to convince him of the usefulness of the scheme.

"You have to admit, it's perfect!" she exclaimed. "You'll be guarding the royal vault, the very vault we need to break into. We couldn't have asked for a better stroke of fortune! You can let us waltz right in and snatch the harp." She giggled rather deviously.

"I suppose," said Elridge, who still looked uncertain. "When am I supposed to start this guard duty?"

"In three days," said Ivy. "That's how long the king said it would take his royal goldsmiths to forge your dragon armor, if they work on it nonstop. I suggested that you start guarding the treasure right away, while the armor was being made, but the king wouldn't hear of it. He said his guards are always suited in gold—and a guard dragon is no exception." Ivy looked at her friend with concern. "You'll be all right out here on your own for a few days, won't you? Owen and I are supposed to move into the castle this evening. Now that we've been granted sanctuary, the royal servants are preparing bedchambers for us and everything. But we can come out and visit you during the day. No one will bother you. The king has made it known that you are now officially in his service."

"Three days," muttered Elridge, shaking his head as if he

couldn't believe he had so little time. "I better practice acting ferocious and guard-dragonly."

Moving into the castle was quite an easy undertaking for Ivy and Owen, seeing as they had brought nothing with them except the clothes on their backs, the compass in Owen's pocket, and the magic mirror tucked into Ivy's boot. But as they walked along the city streets making their way to the castle, Owen expressed as many doubts as Elridge.

"I don't know, Ivy," he said. "I'm a stable boy, not a royal attendant. I don't know if I can play the part. What if I bow at the wrong time, or not at all when I'm supposed to? What if I speak out of turn or say the wrong thing?"

"Owen, you'll be fine," the princess said confidently. "And it's only for three days, so it's not like you have to fool anyone for long. Just do what the other servants do and try to say as little as possible. We'll be leaving for Ardendale as soon as we get our hands on that harp."

When they arrived at the castle, a somber-looking maidservant showed them to their lodgings. Ivy's was a pretty chamber with a canopied bed and a balcony overlooking a small courtyard with a golden fountain.

"Usually, we'd put your lady-in-waiting in the chamber next door, so you could summon her at a moment's notice," said the maid. "But seeing as your servant is a young man, the queen thought it best to house him with the menservants downstairs."

"I'll see you later, Owen," said Ivy. The maid looked startled by this, and Ivy realized that most princesses probably weren't on such friendly terms with their servants. She turned her wave into a brisk shooing motion instead. "I mean, very well, you are dismissed."

Owen looked amused but gave a quick bow before following the maidservant down the hall.

This is great! thought Ivy, shutting the bedchamber door behind them. (It was gold but beaten quite thin, so she could handle it easily.) She didn't know what her friends were so worried about. Snatching the harp was going to be much easier than she'd thought. In the meantime, she'd get to enjoy three days of rest and relaxation inside the golden castle. She sank onto the large bed. Although the frame was made of golden eggs, the mattress was surprisingly soft. She stood and bounced on it a few times, and a handful of white chicken feathers exploded into the air. Ivy laughed.

She plopped down on the mattress and pulled out the magic mirror. "Show me Drusilla's bedchamber again," she commanded. There was a ripple of waves; then Drusilla's airy bedchamber fluttered into view. Even though it was not yet night, the fairy was resting in bed, as Ivy had hoped.

"Drusilla," she called.

"Ivy?" Her godmother sat up at once, turning toward the mirror over her wash basin as if she had been hoping someone would pop in with news. "What's happened? Do you have the harp?"

"Not yet, but soon," promised Ivy. "The king has been a little reluctant to hand it over, but I've got a plan that can't possibly fail. We'll have the harp in three days."

"Three days?" Drusilla looked uneasy. "That's awfully close to Largessa's deadline."

"Don't worry," said Ivy. "It's a quick flight home. Once we have the harp, we'll be there in plenty of time. I need you to tell my father." The princess took a deep, fortifying breath. "And Drusilla, I wanted to say I'm sor—"

She was interrupted by a brisk rap on her bedchamber door.

"Princess Ivory?" came a sharp voice from the other side.

"Fairy cakes, someone's here," she told Drusilla regretfully. "I have to go."

Slipping the mirror back into her boot, Ivy quickly climbed down from the bed. She opened the door to find none other than Master Puckle standing in the hall, wearing the same dark robes and sour expression she had seen earlier. His arms were weighed down by a good dozen books.

"I was told you had been settled in your new chamber," he said stiffly. "I have brought your lesson books."

Without another word, he dumped the pile into her arms. It was so tall and heavy that she had to secure the top of the stack with her chin to keep it from toppling over.

"Lesson books?"

"For your studies," said Master Puckle. "If there is one thing the king cannot stand, it is an uneducated noble. Now that you are a member of his household, you are to be schooled as any other young royal in his care." Master Puckle regarded her darkly, his lips pressed into a reed-thin line. "I suspect, by your lack of knowledge and decorum in the throne room...and elsewhere," his eyes drifted to the feathers on the floor, "that your education in royal matters has been quite deficient. We shall set about correcting this tomorrow morning, first thing after breakfast."

19

Lessons and Lava

These are going to be the worst three days of my life. Ivy slumped against the back of an immensely uncomfortable golden-egg chair in the stuffy, windowless room where Master Puckle held lessons. It was barely midmorning, yet her day already felt abysmally long.

It had started when Owen had knocked on her bedchamber door at a ridiculously early hour.

"It's still dark outside," she had complained as he had lit the candles on her dressing table and filled her basin with water from a golden bucket.

"This is when the royal family arises," he replied, sounding not only wide awake but annoyingly cheerful about it. "You're to have breakfast with them, then attend lessons with Master Puckle. And just so you know, I'm happy to haul your water and carry your books, but I don't do that lady-in-waiting nonsense, so don't expect any help getting dressed." Owen slipped past her and out into the hall.

Ivy blushed hotly at the thought. "I think I can manage to dress myself," she called after his retreating figure. After perusing the dresses in the large golden wardrobe, however, she wasn't so sure. While they weren't as fancy as the gowns she had seen Ninety-Seven and Ninety-Eight wearing, they were far more formal than anything to which she was accustomed. Even the simplest gown she could find had hooks and laces up the back, which she only managed to fasten by bending, stretching, and giving herself a crick in the neck trying to look backward over her shoulder into the mirror.

Breakfast was a formal affair at a golden table in the royal banquet hall. The food was quite good, if you liked golden eggs. There were golden egg omelets, bacon and golden eggs, and golden egg pudding served inside half a golden eggshell. The royal family ate in lofty silence, although the king chewed rather loudly. Ivy had seen birds eat more than the queen and her dainty daughters. Indeed, the queen seemed much more interested in sipping from her golden goblet than in touching anything on her golden plate.

The children of the royal family were all schooled together, so after breakfast Ivy found herself in the lesson room, tucked behind a writing desk between Ninety-Seven and Ninety-Eight, with One-Oh-Three to the far right. Master Puckle stood before them at the front of the room, his expression stern and unsmiling.

"I am going to start by asking you a series of questions to assess your knowledge of royal matters," he said to Ivy. "Etiquette, law, diplomacy, history, and the like."

Ivy wished she could go back to bed and hide beneath the covers.

"If you were introduced to the fifth Duke of Windwell and the third Earl of Ravenwing at a Winterian royal function, whom would you greet first?"

Ivy blinked. "The Duke?" she guessed.

Master Puckle scowled. "Ninety-Seven," he said, "perhaps you could give us the correct answer?"

Ninety-Seven flipped her golden hair over one shoulder with a superior air. "Even though a Duke outranks an Earl, Winterians give age precedence over title. As the third Earl of Ravenwing is forty-three years older than the fifth Duke of Windwell, it would be proper to address the Earl before the Duke."

"Very good," said Master Puckle. "Princess Ivory, which kingdoms signed the Southern North Orsinian Treaty?"

Ivy crinkled her brow. "The what?"

Master Puckle expelled a loud puff of air. "One-Oh-Three?"

"North Orsinia, Boorshire, and the Amaranth Islands," said One-Oh-Three, who looked very sorry for Ivy. "Rosendale pulled out at the last minute as the kingdoms couldn't come to an agreement on the terms of Article Three."

"Correct," said Master Puckle. "Princess Ivory, should a lady being escorted by a Magerian noble stand to his left or to his right?"

"Ummm..."

"Ninety-Eight?" barked Master Puckle, impatiently.

"To his left," said Ninety-Eight, casting a scornful look at Ivy. "In most kingdoms it would be to his right, but the twelfth king of Mageria lost his right arm in a duel against the Thorny Prince of Thistlewood. He escorted ladies on the left by necessity, and that has been the tradition in Mageria ever since."

And so the questioning went on for a good half hour until, at long last, Master Puckle seemed to tire of humiliating her.

"Well," he said, frowning, "this is far worse than I suspected. Princess Ivory, you lack even the most rudimentary elements of a royal education. I can see that we are going to have to implement an intense course of study to correct this. From this day forward, studying is to be the primary focus of your stay in Jackopia. And seeing as Jackopia is your new home, you can start by learning the great history of this most magnificent kingdom." From her pile of lesson books, which Owen had gamely carted down two flights of stairs, Master Puckle selected a tome as large as two or three books put together. He dropped it on Ivy's desk with a bang that made her flinch. *Everything You Need to Know About Jackopia Including a Detailed Chronicle of the Life of Jack the Brave, Mighty, and Truly Magnificent* glittered in gold letters on the cover.

Oh yes, Ivy thought ruefully. *Definitely the worst three days of my life.*

Ivy spent the rest of the morning laboring over the giant tome, while Master Puckle schooled One-Oh-Three, Ninety-Seven, and Ninety-Eight on the finer points of diplomatic negotiation. It was hard to daydream or find distractions around the strict tutor. If Ivy so much as lifted her eyes from the page, Master Puckle fixed her with a look so severe that she immediately dropped her gaze and went back to the task at hand.

Within a short period of time, Ivy was convinced that *Everything You Need to Know About Jackopia Including a Detailed Chronicle of the Life of Jack the Brave, Mighty, and Truly Magnificent* could put even Largessa to sleep. The early chapters were a painfully exhaustive account of Jack's life. According to the book, slaying a giant was only one of his countless brave feats. The others were just as extraordinary—and just as embellished, Ivy suspected. The tale of Jack wrestling a two-headed sea serpent to save a boatload of sick orphans on their way to be cured of prickly pox sounded a bit far-fetched, if you asked her.

Next followed an in-depth history of Jackopia spanning the nearly thousand years from its founding to the present, broken down by reigning monarch. Ivy began to pinch herself beneath her desk, hoping the sharp stabs of pain would keep her awake.

Lunch was a welcome respite, although not a particularly enjoyable one. It was served in the lesson room—golden-egg salad with deviled golden eggs—and once again, everyone ate in well-mannered silence.

After the dishes were cleared, studies resumed. Ivy knew she was likely to collapse of boredom if she had to read about the establishment of one more Jackopian law, so she flipped ahead, desperately hoping there was something remotely interesting in the later chapters.

In a section entitled "The Geography of Jackopia," she actually did discover something of interest—an explanation for the island's oppressive heat:

The glorious golden kingdom of Jackopia nestles within the remnants of an ancient volcano rising from the Speckled Sea. The summit of this volcano was destroyed in a massive eruption centuries ago, forming the basin-shaped island we know today. Lava still flows through the extensive caverns beneath the castle, creating exceedingly warm weather the entire year-round. Locals commonly refer to these caverns as the Burning Between, as they are located beneath the exact center of the island, directly between what is left of the mountain's slopes. The royal forges are located here, as lava is a perfect heat source for melting gold. The Steaming Stream, a large underground river, is also heated by the lava and feeds into the Kettle, a simmering body of water on the surface.

Of course, thought Ivy, the Kettle is the lake outside of town. No wonder it's steaming. And no wonder the island is so warm. The castle is sitting atop a giant bed of lava!

20

A Royal Heart-to-Heart

The only time Ivy had to herself was the few hours before dinner. Master Puckle finally dismissed them from lessons late in the afternoon.

"Out of my way, you stupid oaf," Ninety-Seven snapped at Owen, who had come to collect Ivy's books, entering the doorway just as the golden-haired princess was sweeping out. "Even the most dimwitted peasant knows to let a princess pass before going about his lowly tasks."

"Sorry." Owen bowed his head and stepped aside as Ninety-Seven and Ninety-Eight breezed by. No less than eight elegantly attired ladies-in-waiting had arrived to carry their books and quills, and to cool them with feathered fans lest they break into a sweat strolling the castle halls.

"Sorry, *Your Highness*," Ninety-Seven corrected sharply. "Really, is that what passes for a servant in Ardendale?" she whispered loudly to her sister, as they glided off in a whirl of feathers and fussing attendants. "You'd think he'd never set foot in a castle before. Only a pinheaded simpleton wouldn't know to keep out of the way of his betters."

Owen's cheeks colored, and Ivy felt a surge of anger on his behalf.

"Ignore them," she said. "They're absolute trolls. You should see the nasty looks they've been giving me all day."

"I told you I would be terrible at this," muttered Owen, still staring at the floor.

"Owen, you could never be terrible at anything," Ivy said fiercely. "Those prissy prunes would find fault with the most perfect servant in the world. Like I said, ignore them."

Owen lifted his gaze, his face brightening. "Thanks, Ivy. It means a lot to hear you say so."

Ivy suddenly realized that she and Owen were the last ones in the lesson room, as One-Oh-Three had already left with his gold-armored guard. She was also aware that she was smiling at the stable boy rather stupidly.

"I wanted to visit Elridge, but Master Puckle kept us in lessons all day long," she said, looking away, embarrassed. "I've only got a few hours before dinner with the royal family, and Master Puckle strongly recommends that I spend them reading quietly in my bedchamber. Can you believe it? As if I haven't been reading quietly for the past nine hours!"

"I went to see Elridge this afternoon," said Owen, hoisting her stack of books with a grunt. "Don't worry. He's doing fine."

"Maybe we'll get lucky," Ivy said wistfully. "Maybe the royal goldsmiths will finish the dragon armor early, and we can get out of this stuffy place sooner than planned."

She expected the hours before dinner to drag on as endlessly as the rest of her day, but only minutes after Owen deposited her books in her bedchamber and left to fetch a tray of tea—for all the royals in Jackopia had tea in the afternoon—there was a single, sharp rap on her door.

Ivy assumed that Owen must have forgotten something, but she opened the door to discover none other than the crotchety Captain of the Guard.

"Exactly when did I become the prince's personal message service?" he grumbled under his breath.

"What?" asked Ivy.

The Captain of the Guard cleared his throat. "What I meant to say is, the prince would like to see you in his private sitting chamber . . . again." He gave her an assessing look. "I assume you can find your own way this time?"

"Of course," said Ivy, who didn't want to add to the captain's cranky mood. "It's on the east—no, west side of the castle, past the courtyard with that . . . thing . . . and down the hallway with those . . . other things . . . and up—or down that set of stairs—"

"I'll walk you," said the Captain of the Guard with a sigh.

"That's probably a good idea," said Ivy.

"I'm glad we had a chance to talk before dinner." One-Oh-Three passed the princess a golden teacup. "The tea's lukewarm, as usual," he said, looking a bit embarrassed by this.

"I don't mind," said Ivy, who'd take lukewarm tea over an evening curled up with *Everything You Need to Know About Jackopia Including a Detailed Chronicle of the Life of Jack the Brave, Mighty, and Truly Magnificent* any day.

"I thought Master Puckle was rather hard on you," said One-Oh-Three apologetically, stirring several lumps of sugar into his tea. He had to stir hard; the water wasn't hot enough to dissolve them. "It was only your first day, after all, but Master Puckle can be a bit no-nonsense."

"You don't say." Ivy took a sip of her tea. "I didn't notice."

One-Oh-Three caught her eye, and they both started to laugh. They were seated in the prince's sitting chamber, with one of his ever-present guards keeping watch at the door.

"I wanted to ask you about the royal vault," said Ivy, hoping to take advantage of the prince's light mood. She cast a furtive glance at the guard, but he was out of earshot on the other side of the room. "You know...because my friend Elridge is going to be protecting it."

One-Oh-Three looked uncomfortable. "Actually, I'm not supposed to talk about the royal vault," he said, studying the contents of his teacup rather than meeting her eyes. "Its location is supposed to be secret. Besides the royal family, only the guards and the castle staff that work there know where it is."

Ivy shrugged. It didn't really matter if One-Oh-Three told her the location of the royal vault or not. Elridge would find out soon enough.

"But will you tell me more about Elridge?" One-Oh-Three asked, looking up eagerly. He was suddenly bright-faced behind his spectacles, and Ivy was once again struck by how young and lively he seemed when he wasn't concentrating on sitting up straight and avoiding "unsuitable" topics of conversation. "I probably won't ever get to meet him," the prince said sadly, "but maybe one day he can fly by the castle, and I can at least watch from a window—and maybe he could blow fire! I've always wanted to see a dragon blow fire. When I was small—well, smaller than I am now—I used to think it would be exciting to slay a dragon with a sword, the way Jack the Brave, Mighty, and Truly Magnificent killed the giant. But now I think it would be more fun to do what you do—have a dragon friend who can fly you anywhere and take you on grand adventures!"

"It *is* more fun," said Ivy. "I'm sure Elridge would agree. A prince actually did try to slay him once. Elridge still has a big scar on his side where the prince's spear scraped him." Ivy rubbed the side of her neck thoughtfully. She still had a scar from that unfortunate encounter, too. "It was actually the first time Elridge had ever seen his own blood," she said, her mood lightening as she recalled the dragon's amusingly fainthearted reaction. "Dragon scales are harder than diamonds. Most spears and swords can't pierce them, but this spear was made from a dragon's claw, one of the few things that can cut through dragon hide."

"Wow!" One-Oh-Three's eyes were as wide as saucers. He was on the edge of his seat, his legs dangling a good six inches off the ground.

"I think Elridge would rather forget that it ever happened," said Ivy frankly. "Like you said, flying around is a lot more fun. Not long ago, we flew to this lake on the far side of Ardendale to watch fidget flies dance. It's always fun to see the kingdom from the air. The towns and villages look so small, even smaller than dollhouses."

"I'd like to see a lake one day," said One-Oh-Three, so forlornly that Ivy's heart went out to the diminutive prince. "Or a town. Other than from a window, I mean. And Mother doesn't even like me to stand too close to those."

"One-Oh-Three, are all your days like today?" the princess

asked. "Don't you ever get to do anything but study and sip luke-warm tea?"

"Well sure," said One-Oh-Three, trying to put on a cheerful expression. "Some days Mother lets me watch the royal flower-arranger prepare the centerpiece for the banquet table, as long as I keep a safe distance. Roses have thorns, you know."

Ivy shook her head sadly, and the prince's face fell.

"I know my life must seem boring to you," he said. "I've never befriended a dragon or had to save my kingdom from disaster or flown across the Speckled Sea. I'm certainly no hero like Jack the Brave, Mighty, and Truly Magnificent. But Mother has such terrible nerves. If it wasn't for the calming draught brewed by the royal apothecary, I don't know how she'd manage." Ivy suddenly understood why the queen was always sipping from her golden goblet.

"She'd fall to pieces if she thought I was in any kind of danger," fretted the prince. "Father is always telling me that I mustn't upset her, that I should just concentrate on my studies. He says it's a huge responsibility, ruling an entire kingdom, and that I should prepare for it as much as possible. Rules and books will make me an able king.

"Besides," he added, a little shyly, "maybe my life will be less boring now that you're here. I'll have someone to talk to, for a change. You can tell me about all the exciting things you've done. It will almost be like I've gotten to do them, too."

The princess set down her teacup. "Look, One-Oh-Three, you're right about ruling a kingdom being important. I never took it half as seriously as I should," she admitted with a pang of regret. "But how can your parents expect you to rule a kingdom you've never even seen? You should get out and get to know your people. And everyone—even a crown prince—deserves to have a little fun once in a while."

"I don't know, Ivy," One-Oh-Three said timidly.

"Well, I think you should talk to your parents," said Ivy. "Knowing your kingdom would make you a better king. Surely even they can see the value in that."

"I'll have to think about it," said One-Oh-Three, but his face was slowly brightening again, and his eyes glimmered with the excitement of a new idea.

21

Ridiculous Thoughts

"**I** hope you have been paying careful attention to your reading," Master Puckle said to Ivy the following morning when she was once again ensconced behind a desk in the stuffy lesson room. "Tomorrow I shall test your comprehension of the first forty chapters of *Everything You Need to Know About Jackopia Including a Detailed Chronicle of the Life of Jack the Brave, Mighty, and Truly Magnificent.*"

Ivy felt a plunging sensation deep in the pit of her stomach. "That's over six hundred pages!" she protested.

"As I said, I hope you have been paying careful attention." Master Puckle brushed an invisible piece of lint from his robes. "You will dedicate the rest of the morning to studying. This time, see if you can concentrate longer than a mite-infested hen."

Out of the corner of her eye, Ivy saw Ninety-Seven and Ninety-Eight smirking over the essays they were composing on "My Favorite Jackopian Royal Decree." She tugged at her copy of *Everything You Need to Know About Jackopia Including a Detailed Chronicle of the Life of Jack the Brave, Mighty, and Truly Magnificent*, letting the heavy book fall open with a bang. Ninety-Seven and Ninety-Eight startled at the sound. Ninety-Seven's quill leaped across her parchment, a slash of gold ink ruining her perfect calligraphy.

Both of them glared at Ivy.

"Sorry." The princess smiled sweetly.

After a lunch of pickled golden eggs, Master Puckle ushered his charges to the throne room for another afternoon of royal observation. Ivy thought it proof of how horrendously boring she found lessons that she actually looked forward to spending an afternoon in the company of the Jackopian king.

One-Oh-Three, Ninety-Seven, and Ninety-Eight took their places upon their thrones on the golden dais. The king was already seated on his cushion, and the queen was sipping delicately from yet another golden goblet.

Someone had dragged forth a lumpy golden-egg stool so that Ivy could sit to one side of the dais, next to none other than Master Puckle.

"Pay attention and you might actually learn something," the tutor said snootily.

It was a good thing that her copy of *Everything You Need to Know About Jackopia Including a Detailed Chronicle of the Life of Jack the Brave, Mighty, and Truly Magnificent* was back in the lesson room, thought Ivy. Otherwise, she might have been tempted to throw it at him.

It was just as warm in the throne room as she remembered,

but servants provided some relief with large feathered fans. Owen, standing to Ivy's side, did his best to keep her cool with an enormous fan nearly as tall as he.

"Do you mind?" snapped Ninety-Seven, who was sitting at the end of the dais, closest to Ivy. "Can't you do something as simple as wave a fan? You're supposed to create a gentle breeze, not stir up a windstorm. I can feel it all the way over here. It's messing up my hair."

Owen immediately dropped his gaze to the golden floor. "I-I'm sorry, Your Highness."

"So you should be," huffed Ninety-Seven, smoothing her lustrous locks.

"It's all right, Owen," Ivy spoke up quickly, eyes shooting daggers at Ninety-Seven. "You can stop now. I'm perfectly comfortable, thank you."

"I suppose some princesses don't care if they develop an unsightly glisten," Ninety-Seven made a point of remarking to her sister.

A very unflattering reply rose to Ivy's lips, but she bit her tongue when Master Puckle fixed her with a disapproving frown.

"Children, you are in for a treat today!" said the Jackopian king, raising a ring-studded hand for their attention. "This afternoon is my semiweekly meeting with the royal egg-countants. Oh, how I love talking about how much gold is in the royal vault!"

The royal vault. Ivy sat up a little straighter. The afternoon might not be a complete waste after all.

"Father," One-Oh-Three said tentatively, pushing his spectacles farther up on his nose. "Before we begin, may I ask you a question?"

"Of course you may, my boy," the king said cheerfully. "Is it about gold?"

"Yes. I mean, no. I mean...sort of, but not really." One-Oh-Three wrung his hands nervously.

"Well, gold is my favorite subject, but you know I'm always happy to answer any question you may have." The king smiled fondly at his young son.

"The thing is, it's almost Monarch's Day," said One-Oh-Three.

"Ah yes," said the king. "My favorite holiday, when I do my yearly inspection of the city. We can't have any of those golden eggs cracking and leaving unsightly marks on our beautiful buildings, now can we? And when that's done, the people will hold a huge feast in my honor." He rubbed his hands together eagerly. "I can't wait. It's only two days away."

"Every year, you and Mother and Ninety-Seven and Ninety-Eight attend the festivities in the city. And I thought maybe this year," said One-Oh-Three, his voice very soft, "that perhaps...I could go with you."

A shocked silence fell over the throne room, broken only when the queen dropped her golden goblet and several servants rushed forward to attend to the spill.

"Come again, my boy?" The king's mustache twitched. "I don't think I heard you correctly. I thought you asked if you could accompany us into the city."

"I did," said One-Oh-Three, speaking a little louder. He shot a sideways glance at Ivy, as if hoping this would lend him courage. "I think it would be good for me and help with my studies. I mean, how can I rule a kingdom I've never even seen?"

The queen suddenly burst into tears. "One-Oh-Three,

146

th-this is very inconsiderate of you!" she cried, her voice so high-pitched it made Ivy cringe. "You k-know I can't s-stand the thought of you in d-danger. Do you have any idea wh-what this is doing to my nerves? I need more calming draught—quickly!" She snapped her fingers frantically, and a servant rushed forward with a golden tray bearing two more goblets.

"Son, you know leaving the castle is out of the question," the king said sternly.

"The w-world is such a p-perilous place," sobbed the queen, "and you're such a s-small and delicate boy. You could g-get hurt." Greatly distressed by the thought, she quickly drained one goblet from the tray and reached for the other.

"I didn't mean to upset you, Mother," said One-Oh-Three. "I just don't see what could possibly happen to me in the city."

"It could rain, and you c-could catch your death of a cold," said the queen.

Ivy nearly snorted. She doubted it had rained on this bone-dry island in years.

"You could be c-crushed by a runaway c-cart," continued the queen, taking several swallows from the fresh goblet and fanning herself furiously with her lace handkerchief. Her voice dropped to a whisper, as if she were sharing a terrible secret. "And th-there are *wild animals* out there."

Ivy's jaw dropped in disbelief. Since arriving in Jackopia, she hadn't seen anything wilder than a white hen.

"Oh, what w-would I do if s-something happened to you?" wailed the queen, sounding near-hysterical. She gulped the remaining contents of the goblet. "Oh, my d-dear, sweet boy. H-how would I g-go on?"

"There, there, Hortensia." The king laid a comforting hand

on the arm of his weeping wife. "There's no need to upset your-self so. We'll keep the boy safe, I promise." He turned to his son. "One-Oh-Three, you know your mother feels that you should not leave the castle until you are bigger and stronger," he said.

"But Father, I might not ever get bigger or stronger," pro-tested One-Oh-Three. "I've hardly grown at all these last few years. And I think it's important that I get to know the people. After all, knowing my kingdom will make me a better king."

"You don't have to *know* people to rule over them," scoffed his father. "You just tell them what to do, and they do it. That's what being king is all about. Get to know the people, *pshaw.* Who is putting such ridiculous thoughts in your head?" Almost as soon as the words were out of his mouth, he turned and gave Ivy a dark, suspicious glare.

"It's not like One-Oh-Three is made of glass," the princess said defiantly, meeting his gaze. "He's not going to break if a but-terfly brushes up against him."

"Someone like you wouldn't understand," the queen said weakly. The large quantities of draught looked to be taking effect. She seemed calmer now but very sleepy. Her eyelids were starting to droop, and she swayed on her throne. "My boy is far ... too ... fragile ... for ... such ... things."

"One-Oh-Three is stronger than you give him credit for," said Ivy, "and it's about time he saw the world outside these cas-tle walls."

"Hogwash," said the king in a voice that broached no argu-ment, "and I'll thank you not to fill my son's head with such silly notions."

He turned to One-Oh-Three, his face as grave as Ivy had ever seen. "Now just look at what you've done to your poor mother. This unpleasantness has been more than her nerves can bear." The queen's head had lolled to one side. Her eyes were closed, and her mouth was hanging open, releasing a series of loud, rather unladylike snores. The king fixed his son with a serious gaze. "Attending the Monarch's Day celebration is out of the question, One-Oh-Three, and I don't ever, *ever* want to hear another word about you leaving the castle. You'll leave the castle when your mother and I see fit, and not a moment before. Is that understood?"

One-Oh-Three hung his head. "Yes, Father," he said meekly. Ivy wouldn't have thought it possible for him to look any smaller, but at that moment, he seemed more diminutive than ever. Her heart went out to him.

22

Night Flight

"Don't flap so hard," Ivy whispered to Elridge. "Your wings make a lot of noise. And stay away from those windows. I think that's the hallway outside the armory. It'll be busy with guards, even this time of night."

"Good goat fur, you're making me nervous," Elridge whispered back. But he did as Ivy requested and steered away from the long row of windows, sticking to the shadows along the castle's uppermost heights. With his dark coloring, Elridge blended in with the night. When there was no light bouncing off his shiny scales, he was hard to spot.

"There." Ivy pointed to one of the lofty towers. "I'm pretty sure that's One-Oh-Three's bedchamber."

"Pretty sure?" Elridge swung his head around and gave her a doubtful look.

"Well, it's a big castle," Ivy said defensively. She was a bit grouchy because she had spent the entire afternoon in a meeting with the royal egg-countants and had learned nothing about the royal vault, except the number of golden eggs it contained (one million, five hundred thousand, one hundred eighty-two) and the number it was expected to contain by the end of the week (one million, five hundred thousand, nine hundred fifty-four). "Sometimes it's hard to find your way around. But I know he has a whole tower to himself, and the servants who bring his wash water always turn down the north hallway on the fourth floor, so yes, that has to be it. It's the only tower on this side of the castle."

"I guess we'll find out," said Elridge. "But you said he slept with a guard outside his door. We could get caught."

"The guard is outside his *door*, not his window," reasoned Ivy. "As long as we're quiet, we should be okay."

Elridge glided to the large open window at the top of the tower in question. Not surprisingly, it was dark. Most of the castle had long been asleep, but Ivy leaned forward and whispered a sharp, "One-Oh-Three! One-Oh-Three, come to the window. It's Ivy."

The third time she called his name, she heard the striking of a flame, and the chamber flooded with pale, flickering light. One-Oh-Three appeared in the window, clutching a lighted candlestick in one hand and shoving his spectacles onto his face with the other.

"Ivy? What are you doing outside my window? It's the middle of the night." One-Oh-Three looked puzzled and half asleep. Then he spotted Elridge, and his eyes grew huge. "Whoa!"

"Put that candle out—quickly!" whispered Ivy. "Someone will see us."

One-Oh-Three fumbled with the candle, extinguishing it with a puff of breath.

"I can't believe it," he whispered in the darkness, his voice dangerously close to not being a whisper at all. "You brought your dragon friend! There's a real-live dragon, right here, outside my bedchamber window!"

"One-Oh-Three, Elridge," said Ivy, who couldn't help but be pleased by the prince's reaction. "Elridge, One-Oh-Three."

"Hello," Elridge said in a friendly tone.

"I-I never thought I'd get to see a dragon," gushed One-Oh-Three, his voice brimming with excitement. "Leaping lava, this is amazing!"

"Nice to meet you, too," said Elridge, quite flattered.

One-Oh-Three's eyes had apparently adjusted to the darkness. He was leaning out of the window, taking in Elridge's impressive form in the murky moonlight.

"Well, don't just stand there gaping," said Ivy, laughing. "Take my hand and climb on. Be careful now." She offered her hand to the wide-eyed prince.

One-Oh-Three looked ready to burst out of his skin. "You don't mean..."

"That's right," said Ivy. "We're taking you for a ride. Since you couldn't come to the dragon, we've brought the dragon to you."

"Ivy, we've been gone a long time," said Elridge, making a wide circle over the steaming lake, away from the peaked rooftops of the city. "Shouldn't we get back to the castle before someone notices that One-Oh-Three is missing?"

"Just a few more minutes," said Ivy. "Come on, Elridge, it's not like One-Oh-Three's going to have another chance to ride a dragon. Or even leave the castle anytime soon."

"Oh yes, please, Elridge," pleaded One-Oh-Three. "This is incredible. I can't believe I'm actually flying on a dragon. I never knew the city was so big and beautiful, and I've always wanted to see the Kettle, and there are so many fountains in the city's squares. I bet they look amazing when they're all sparkly in the sunlight. Oh, this is the best night ever!" The young prince sighed and rested his head contentedly against the dragon spine he was clutching.

Ivy, sitting behind him, gave a cheerful laugh. "I'm glad you like it. Like I said, everyone deserves to have a little fun. And I think it was really brave of you to talk to your parents today."

"But it didn't work out so well, did it," One-Oh-Three said sadly. "To think you get to do things like this all the time. My life is so unbelievably boring."

His voice was heavy with regret, and Ivy found that she shared it.

"The truth is I've probably spent a little too much time soaring around the clouds," she told him. "I wish I knew half as much about ruling a kingdom as you do. I wouldn't have even known to ask for sanctuary if you hadn't told me. I didn't take my responsibilities seriously, but you're not like that at all. One-Oh-Three, you're going to be a wonderful king."

This didn't seem to cheer the young prince. "You can always study more," he pointed out matter-of-factly. "I'm stuck in the castle, and my life isn't likely to get any more exciting."

"I don't know," said Ivy. "In my experience, you can usually find excitement if you go looking for it."

"Speaking of going," said Elridge, "I really think we should head back to the castle. The sun will be up soon."

Ivy hadn't noticed, but the sky was lightening. Soon there

would be touches of pink blossoming in the east. Elridge set course for the castle, soaring high over the city. The castle still looked quiet as they approached, but as Elridge ascended the northern tower, Ivy heard a familiar voice ringing out in the predawn air.

"I see him—I see him, Your Majesty!"

Ivy's heartbeat quickened. Hanging out of the prince's high bedchamber window was the gold-helmeted head of the Captain of the Guard, his fierce gaze locked upon them.

"Oh no," One-Oh-Three groaned.

"Oh no is right," gulped Elridge. But they had been spotted, and there was no turning back now. The dragon drew up to the window in a fluid motion, and the Captain of the Guard seized the prince's arm in his brawny grasp, guiding the boy inside. Ivy climbed in after.

"One-Oh-Three!" cried the queen, dropping the golden goblet in her grasp. She hurtled forward and snatched the prince in her arms, sobbing hysterically. "Oh, my d-dear boy, my d-dear, dear boy," she wailed. "I th-thought I'd lost you, th-thought I'd never s-see you again."

Ivy was dismayed to find that the room was packed with people—not only the king and queen, but Master Puckle, the Captain of the Guard, and a number of gold-clad guards and fussing servants, a fair number still in their nightclothes. The queen was in a lavender dressing gown.

"Mother?" One-Oh-Three looked shocked. "What are you doing here?"

The queen was still sobbing uncontrollably. Her tear-stained eyes drifted past her son, toward the window, and she gasped in horror.

"Is th-that the d-d-dragon?" she asked in a weak, fluttery

voice. "Did y-you just g-get off that...d-d-dragon?" Her eyes rolled back into her head, and she dropped in a dead faint, servants rushing forward to catch her in their arms.

"Hortensia!" cried the king. Then he turned to Ivy. His lips were pressed thin, his face white with fury. "How dare you," he screamed. "How dare you take my son from this castle!"

23

A (Not-So) Fitting Punishment

Ivy and One-Oh-Three stood in the main courtyard of the castle, in front of the gate to the drawbridge, watching as the king of Jackopia paced back and forth across the golden cobblestones. He had been at it for some time, and it was slow going given his heavy girth. The princess had his routine memorized: eight steps toward the western wall of the courtyard, pause and spin, eight steps toward the eastern wall, pause and spin, and start over again.

"I think I'm about to get kicked out of your kingdom," she risked whispering to One-Oh-Three when the king's back was turned.

"He can't kick you out," the prince whispered back. "Remember? He *has* to give you sanctuary. It's the law."

Master Puckle shot them a venomous look from where he stood stiffly next to the Captain of the Guard, and both fell silent again.

The king had requested that Elridge be present in the court-yard as well, the first time the dragon had been invited inside the castle walls.

That can't be good, thought Ivy, watching the dragon shuffle his claws and glance nervously at his surroundings, as if he expected a battalion of gold-armored guards to storm the court-yard at any moment, intent on attack.

They wouldn't hurt Elridge, she tried to reassure herself.

Owen stood with Elridge and rested a comforting hand on the dragon's scaly side.

Finally, the king halted his furious march and came to a stop before Ivy and One-Oh-Three.

"How could you, One-Oh-Three?" he asked his son, his voice a mix of anger and hurt. "How could you leave the castle when I expressly forbade you from doing so? And what would possess you to do something as reckless as fly on the back of a fire-breathing reptile?"

"I guess I didn't think there was any harm in it," One-Oh-Three replied, dropping his gaze.

"No harm in it?" The king's eyes widened in disbelief. "Do you realize that you could have fallen? That you could have been killed?"

"I-I'm sorry, Father," said One-Oh-Three. "I wasn't thinking."

"You certainly weren't." The king gave an agitated tug on his mustache. "Do you have any idea what this has done to your poor mother's nerves? When your night guard found your bed empty during his hourly check, the entire castle was in an uproar."

"Wait a minute," said One-Oh-Three, raising his head, startled. "The guard looks in on me? While I'm *asleep?*"

"Every hour on the hour," the king said matter-of-factly. "You know your mother is afraid you'll stop breathing in your sleep."

One-Oh-Three looked a bit indignant at this but held his tongue, probably guessing that this was not the best time to question the actions of his parents.

"The royal healers have had to give her so much calming draught, it'll be a miracle if she doesn't sleep for two days straight," continued the king. "I fear she may never recover from the shock."

"I'm sorry, Father," One-Oh-Three repeated, his head bowed, his face pale with shame.

The king studied his son with a somber expression, the lines on his face deepening.

"Well, we must do something to soothe your mother's frazzled nerves, to reassure her that such a thing will never happen again," he said. "Apparently, you cannot be trusted to stay in the castle on your own, so from this day forth, a guard will be with you at all times—*all* times—whether you are sleeping, eating, studying, bathing. There will be no exceptions."

One-Oh-Three flushed red, and Ivy felt exceedingly sorry for him. She couldn't imagine how humiliating it was to be treated like a helpless toddler who couldn't even sleep or bathe on his own.

"As for you"—the king speared Ivy with a searing gaze— "you are no longer allowed to spend time with my son, unless the two of you are in the same room together, with others present, for meals or lessons. I can't force you from this castle, but I can ensure that you will behave while here. I can see that you are used to having far too much freedom. It has made you wild and undisciplined. You must remain in a structured environment where your behavior can be monitored. Therefore, you yourself are no longer allowed outside the castle. That should help keep you out of trouble." The king gave her a triumphant smile. "Of course, if being confined to the castle is not to your liking, you are most welcome to quit our shores entirely."

Ivy felt blood rising to her face, and angry words sprang to the tip of her tongue. It took all the resolve she had not to unleash them with a vengeance. *The harp,* she reminded herself, balling her fists in frustration. *I need to stay to find the harp.*

"Fine," she ground out through clenched teeth. "I won't leave the castle."

The king looked disappointed by this. He shifted his attention to Elridge.

"By all rights, I should cast you from my kingdom immediately," he said. "I am only allowing you to stay because the royal goldsmiths have completed your armor, and I hate for the fruits of their labor to go to waste." He nodded briskly at the Captain of the Guard, who in turn shouted, "Bring forth the royal dragon armor!"

The courtyard was promptly flooded with a dozen armored guards, bearing large pieces of molded gold. Ivy had to admit that the armor was quite impressive, its gleaming surface covered with hundreds of overlapping scales that mimicked Elridge's own.

"If you are still prepared to guard my royal vault, I will overlook last night's grievous transgression," said the king, as if he was doing Elridge a great favor.

Elridge shot a glance at Ivy, who nodded. As much as it pained her to go along with the king's self-important plans, they still needed to uncover the location of the royal vault.

"Of course, Your Majesty." Elridge acquiesced, lying on all fours so that the guards could affix the armor.

It was fashioned in two large pieces. One fit over the spines on Elridge's back and covered his sides like a half shell, fastening with long leather straps that ran beneath his belly. The royal goldsmiths knew nothing about dragons, Ivy decided. Elridge's soft underbelly was his most vulnerable spot, not the parts of him already covered with his own diamond-hard scales.

The other piece was a magnificent helmet with golden spikes that made it look as if Elridge had grown six new horns, in addition to the two he already had.

Guards bustled about the dragon while he anxiously watched them fit and fasten the armor into place. Finally, two of the guards positioned the helmet, fumbling with fastenings at either side of the mouthpiece. They appeared to be attaching long lengths of gold chain.

"What's the chain for?" Ivy asked.

"Hey," said Elridge, sounding very muffled. "This helmet is on too tight. I can barely open my mouth."

A sense of unease gave way to shock as Ivy realized that Elridge had just been muzzled. The dragon must have grasped this as well, for he jerked his head and jolted to his feet. The chains dangled like a horse's reins, with nine guards seizing hold and pulling with all their might, preventing the dragon from escaping.

"What are you doing?" shouted the princess. She made to dash forward, but an armored hand clamped down on her shoulder. She looked up into the grim face of the Captain of the Guard.

"It would be best if you didn't interfere," he said briskly.

Elridge was thrashing like mad. He flapped his wings, but they were useless while he was weighed down by the gold and the guards. The thick helmet covered his nostrils, preventing him from breathing fire, but there was still his tail. Elridge lashed it around wildly, overturning a stack of golden barrels that had been piled in the corner of the courtyard.

Several guards drew their swords.

"No!" screamed Ivy. She was still locked in the iron grip of the Captain of the Guard. She aimed a well-placed kick at his left shin, which, unfortunately, did nothing but clang off his armor and painfully bruise her big toe.

"You said you were going to overlook what happened!" she shouted at the king.

"And so I am," he replied calmly. "I didn't expel the dragon from my kingdom, did I? But the beast has proven too much of a risk to roam free. He'll be chained in front of the vault, where his presence will dissuade would-be thieves. That way, my guards can keep an eye on him. He'll not have the opportunity to endanger my son again."

The guards were now forcing Elridge from the courtyard. Some tugged the gold chains linked to his helmet, while others prodded him with swords to move him along.

Ivy wanted to cry. She also had the powerful urge to strike the king with her fist. Thankfully, before she could do anything too rash, Owen was at her side, slipping a comforting arm around her, holding her in place. The Captain of the Guard finally released his grasp.

"It's all right," Owen whispered in her ear, his breath warm against her hair. "We'll save him. I promise. We'll find the royal vault and save him."

The king watched coldly as the dragon was dragged through the castle gate, a look of grim satisfaction on his flabby face. "A fitting punishment, I think, for what has been done."

Master Puckle made Ivy and One-Oh-Three return to the lesson room for an afternoon of studies. He rather generously postponed quizzing the princess on the first forty chapters of *Everything You Need to Know About Jackopia Including a Detailed Chronicle of the Life of Jack the Brave, Mighty, and Truly Magnificent*.

"I'm guessing you didn't get much studying done last night," he remarked dryly.

Ivy spent the rest of the afternoon pretending to read. She was sick with worry about Elridge, and the words on the pages kept blurring before her eyes.

Her situation had become very grave indeed. Largessa's deadline was rapidly approaching, and she still had no idea where the royal vault was located. She was stuck in this clammy little room with Master Puckle, poring over a ridiculous book when she should be hunting for the royal vault.

That's it, she thought desperately. *Tonight, I'm scouring this stupid castle from top to bottom until I find that blasted vault. I'll stay up all night if I have to.*

One-Oh-Three kept shooting discreet glances her way while hunched over his own assignments, clearly wanting to talk to her. But while a guard had always shown up to escort him to and from lessons before, now one sat in an extra desk directly behind him, a result of the king's new command. There was no way One-Oh-Three could have had a quiet word with her, no matter how much he wanted to.

The young prince must have been just as distracted as Ivy by the day's events, for when Master Puckle released them late in the afternoon, he knocked into her desk on his way out the door, spilling her pile of lesson books to the floor just as Owen arrived to collect them.

"Sorry," he said softly. Not meeting her eyes, he handed her the book that had fallen at his feet. Owen set about gathering the rest as the prince hurried off with his guard.

"Poor One-Oh-Three," said Owen. "He looks miserable. I bet he feels terrible about Elridge getting locked up."

Ivy didn't answer. She was staring at the book in her hands, for there was a scrap of cream-colored parchment poking out from the pages. She slipped it out and unfolded the crease. Immediately, she recognized One-Oh-Three's tiny handwriting, scribbled in haste, not nearly as tidy as the summons he had sent her a few days ago. The message was brief but significant:

Royal vault is beneath the castle, past the forges,
inside the Burning Between.

PART THREE

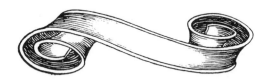

The Burning Between
and Back Again

24

Descent

"Word among the servants is that the entrance to the forges is near the Hen Hive," said Owen. As he and Ivy made their way down the narrow stairs to the lower level of the castle, they were beset by waves of air even warmer than the rest of the island. "It makes it easy to transport the golden eggs there. The forges and the vault are both in the Burning Between, so if we can get to one—"

"—we can get to the other," finished Ivy. She thought it very clever of Owen to have picked up this useful bit of information. "And once we're at the vault, we'll find both Elridge and the harp." She peered down the stairs, pleased that her surroundings looked familiar. "Well, this is definitely the way to the Hen Hive." The princess was amazed that she had managed to recall the route at all. Desperation had apparently sharpened her memory. "There's a room inside the Hive where cartloads of golden eggs are sorted. They're probably wheeled to the vault from there."

Halfway down the stairs, she paused, struck by a thought she had been too harried to consider before. "There'll be guards in front of the door to the Hive, even at this time of night. I don't know how we can find the way to the forges without being seen."

"I know where they are," a voice drifted from the shadows at the top of the stairs, making Ivy jump. "Down the hall from the entrance to the Hive is a platform attached to a pulley. That's where workers and carts are lowered into the Burning Between."

"One-Oh-Three!" Ivy turned to see the coppery-haired prince descending the stairs toward them. "What are you doing here?"

"I overheard your plan to find the royal vault and save Elridge," said One-Oh-Three. "I was standing next to you in the courtyard when Owen whispered to you. My hearing's pretty good." The prince looked at the pair hopefully. "I want to help. That's why I told you the location of the vault."

"But how did you get here? There's supposed to be a guard with you at all times."

"Well, I actually, kind of...managed to get away from him," One-Oh-Three said hesitantly, as if he wasn't sure how they would react to this. "About a month ago I had a bit of a cough, and Mother sat with me the whole night." His cheeks colored with embarrassment. "She left a vial of calming draught in my bedchamber. I tossed it in the back of my wardrobe, and it's been there ever since. When I invited my guard to have a cup of tea with me this evening, I poured calming draught into his teacup. My tea is never hot anyway, so he didn't notice the difference. He'll be asleep for hours. The draught's really strong, especially when you're not used to it." One-Oh-Three looked quite proud of his feat; his eyes shone bright behind the lenses of his spectacles.

"That was really clever," said Ivy, and indeed, she was greatly impressed by the prince's resourcefulness. "But the king will be furious if he finds out you left your bedchamber without your guard. Maybe you should get back before he wakes up."

"Absolutely not," said One-Oh-Three, his face firm with resolve. Suddenly, he didn't seem quite so young or so small. "It's my fault Elridge was chained up. I think it terribly unfair that Father imprisoned him just because he was nice enough to fly me around the kingdom a bit. The least I can do is help rescue him."

Ivy and Owen exchanged glances.

"I don't think that's such a good idea, One-Oh-Three," said Ivy.

"I know a lot about the Burning Between," offered the prince. "It was part of my studies. For instance, I know there's another exit from the caverns, one that leads outside. That's the way the guards would have brought Elridge in, and it's the only way you're getting him out. He's too big and heavy for the platform and pulley."

Ivy hadn't thought of this. They did need an escape route. Perhaps it *would* be useful to have someone with them who knew the lay of the land.

"Ivy, we can't take him with us." Owen, as if reading her thoughts, leaned forward to whisper in her ear. "What about"—he lowered his voice even further—"the *harp?*"

"The harp?" One-Oh-Three looked from one to the other, puzzled. "What about the harp?"

The young prince apparently *did* have extraordinarily sharp hearing.

Suddenly, Ivy was struck by an immense wave of guilt. One-Oh-Three had risked his father's wrath to meet them here. He was so eager to help save Elridge, with no idea that doing so would involve him in a plot to steal one of his own kingdom's royal treasures.

He deserves better, she thought with a heavy heart. *I have to tell him the truth.*

"One-Oh-Three, I haven't been honest with you," she admitted. "I was never planning to stay in Jackopia. The only reason I asked for sanctuary was to buy myself time to find the royal vault. It was my plan all along to steal the harp."

Behind his large spectacles, One-Oh-Three blinked. "You want to steal the harp?"

"I don't *want* to, exactly," said Ivy. "I mean, I don't really have a choice, do I? It's the only way to save my kingdom."

One-Oh-Three didn't answer, and Ivy groaned inwardly. Maybe being truthful with him hadn't been the wisest course of action. He looked stunned and hurt and betrayed, perhaps betrayed enough to reveal their plot to the king.

"I'm really sorry to have misled you," she added quickly. "I know you must be terribly disappointed in me. But when your father refused to give me the harp, I didn't know what else to do."

"It's okay, Ivy," One-Oh-Three said, his shock fading and his face softening. "You don't have to explain. If my kingdom was in danger, I would probably do the same thing. It is only a harp, after all. Taking it isn't going to hurt anyone, and it could save a lot of lives."

Ivy breathed a sigh of relief. "So you see why you can't come with us? You'd get in terrible trouble—not just for helping to free Elridge but for helping us steal the harp."

Once again, One-Oh-Three's face grew determined. "I don't care," he declared. "Jack the Brave, Mighty, and Truly Magnificent didn't just stand around while people were in danger, and I'm not going to, either. Besides," he added with a small grin, "someone once told me you can usually find excitement if you go looking for it—and this is definitely going to be exciting!"

The enormous pillars at the bottom of the stairs proved a great hiding place from the two guards outside the Hen Hive. Unfortunately, Ivy, Owen, and One-Oh-Three seemed to be trapped there.

"How are we going to make it down the hall without being seen?" Ivy whispered to her friends, frowning. There were a few workers exiting the Hive with carts, even at this late hour, but the three of them hardly blended in.

"I can't be seen down here," fretted the princess. "The king has probably warned all of his guards to keep an eye on me, so it's not like I can show up at the Hen Hive in the middle of the night without arousing suspicion."

"Me, neither," said One-Oh-Three with a sigh. "The crown prince, by himself, without an escort. That'll send up a red flag for sure."

They fell silent as a small group of workers wheeled carts full of golden eggs past the pillar where they crouched.

"Going to be a long night," one worker observed, "what with Hector sick. All the more work for us."

"Hmmm," mused Owen, as the carts continued down the hall. "Maybe two royals would stand out like sore thumbs, but no one would think twice about seeing a lowly servant."

Ivy's heart froze as the stable boy rose to his feet and stepped out into the open. She heard his steady footfalls move away from the pillar.

"I've been asked to help out tonight," came his voice, and Ivy knew he must be speaking to the guards in front of the Hive's entrance. "You know, because Hector's sick."

Ivy's breath caught in her throat, but she needn't have worried.

"It's a good thing you're here," one of the guards replied agreeably. "The hens are laying like mad tonight. I think another cart has already been started. Just pile in some more eggs, and you'll be good to go."

There was a scrape as the golden doors to the Hive were heaved open.

"What about us?" Ivy whispered to One-Oh-Three with concern. "Now Owen can get into the Burning Between, but what are we supposed to do?"

Her question was answered about ten minutes later, when voices traveled up the hall, along with the creaking of cart wheels. The workers were returning, back for another load. She heard the golden doors heave open again.

"Thanks," said Owen, who must have been on his way out.

"Look, Artus, you've been sent some extra help." It was the guard who had spoken earlier.

"Excellent," replied one of the workers. "Head on down to the vault, son. Thomas is manning the pulley. We'll join you just as soon as we fill our carts again."

"Hey, Dunston," said another worker, apparently addressing the guard. "How's that pretty new wife of yours?"

It seemed the workers were not in any great hurry to resume their tasks, as a very leisurely conversation ensued.

"*Psssst.*"

Ivy started; the sound came directly from the other side of the pillar. "I didn't fill the cart the whole way," whispered Owen. "There's still lots of room. Get in quick, while the guards are busy talking."

Cautiously, Ivy peeked out. The guards at the entrance of the Hen Hive were indeed deep in conversation with the group of workers. Taking One-Oh-Three by the sleeve, Ivy dragged him around the pillar, where Owen waited with a large golden cart. Hitching her skirts about her knees, she tugged herself up and over the side. In her haste, she landed hard atop a lumpy bed of golden eggs.

Ouch! She bit her lip and rubbed her backside.

A moment later, One-Oh-Three joined her, helped by Owen. Ivy wished golden eggs weren't so heavy and noisy. It would have been nice to burrow beneath them, hidden from view, but she worried the clatter would attract the guards.

"Here we go," Owen whispered. The cart began to move, and the voices outside the Hen Hive faded into the distance.

They were rolling down a dim, windowless hallway. From her position inside the cart, Ivy could only make out the ceiling and the golden torches along the walls. There was a terrible stench in the air, growing stronger by the moment. Ivy covered her nose with her sleeve as the cart creaked to a stop.

"Are you Thomas?" Owen asked someone Ivy couldn't see. "I'm helping out for the night. Artus said to see you."

"Wheel your cart onto the platform there," instructed the man called Thomas. "I'll lower you down—and don't worry now. This pulley and platform are very cleverly constructed. They'll take the weight of a cartload of golden eggs. Never been to the royal vault before, have you? Just follow the passage at the bottom, past the forges, to the very end."

The cart heaved forward again. The rattle of the wheels was different, a little hollow-sounding, as if the ground was not quite solid beneath them. The princess knew they must be on the platform.

"Don't know if you heard," said Thomas, "but the king staked a dragon outside the vault just this afternoon. Don't be afraid when you see him. He's fettered by some good solid chains. Doesn't seem a particularly ferocious beast, in any case, if you ask me. The guards outside the vault will let you in."

With a groan, the platform lowered beneath them. The air grew even warmer and darker, the smell so rancid that Ivy's eyes began to water. As hard as she tried, the princess couldn't shake the ominous feeling that they were descending directly into the maw of some putrid-breathed monster.

25

The Royal Vault

It was nearly dark at the bottom of the platform. There were torches here, too, but they were widely spaced, emitting only feeble casts of flickering light. The stone walls told Ivy that they were underground. It felt like the inside of an oven. After only a few moments, Ivy's dress was clinging in patches to her damp skin. To make matters worse, the smell here was almost unbearable, the air rank with a stench like rotten eggs.

"Leaping lava, it stinks," complained One-Oh-Three, covering his nose with his hand.

"Lava is right," said Owen, awestruck. "There's a huge pool of it. The royal goldsmiths are using it to melt gold in enormous cauldrons. Wow! We've definitely found the forges."

Indeed, Ivy could hear the clanks and clangs of hammers on anvils, and the indistinct rumble of men's voices. Apparently, work in the royal forges didn't stop at night. There was also what sounded like a rushing river.

"Are we near water?" she asked, perplexed.

"Yes," said Owen, "right next to the path we're on. But I wouldn't venture a swim. It's hot as a cooking pot. The lava must heat it."

"That's the Steaming Stream," One-Oh-Three said knowingly.

Ivy remembered now. *Everything You Need to Know About Jackopia Including a Detailed Chronicle of the Life of Jack the Brave, Mighty, and Truly Magnificent* had mentioned the stream that fed into the Kettle.

"You're going to have to be quiet now," said Owen, lowering his own voice. "There are goldsmiths around, and this passage leads to the royal vault. There'll be more guards there."

Ivy nodded, even though she knew Owen couldn't see. The cart rolled onward, away from the busy sounds of the forges. It rattled around a bend, where the dimness washed away in a flood of golden light.

Owen gasped.

From her hiding place inside the cart, Ivy could just make out the top of what appeared to be an enormous golden door, stretching to the ceiling. There was so much gold, it gave off a brilliant glow even in the meager torchlight.

The entrance to the vault!

Owen pushed the cart forward. "I see Elridge—and the guards," he whispered urgently, under his breath.

Ivy hunkered down, golden eggs pushing uncomfortably into her skin. The giant door drew closer and closer, soon taking up nearly her entire field of view.

"More golden eggs for the vault," Owen said casually, and Ivy guessed he was talking to the guards.

She couldn't see what was happening, but there was the jangle of keys and a series of clicks like a dozen locks being unbolted, and then the gigantic door swung open, just wide enough for the cart to be wheeled through.

"Thanks," said Owen, starting forward.

The light was just as bright inside the vault. There were torches and tons of gold here, too. In fact, Ivy could see the pointed summits of what looked like veritable mountains of golden eggs. The door swung closed behind them with a thud that resounded off the stone walls.

"Okay, you can come out now," said Owen, sounding hugely relieved.

Ivy tentatively poked her head over the edge of the cart. She could see that they were in an enormous cavern, surrounded by massive piles of golden eggs. Scattered about were other treasures, as well. Several solid gold statues of Jack the Brave, Mighty, and Truly Magnificent posed heroically. Open chests displayed diadems and jewels. A five-foot-wide gold replica of a ship with towering masts sailed the sea of eggs.

Owen's done it! Ivy thought excitedly. *He's gotten us inside the royal vault!*

"Oh dear," said One-Oh-Three, struggling to climb out of the cart behind Ivy. "It's not going to be easy, finding the harp in all this."

"How did Elridge look?" asked Ivy with concern.

"Shackled down with a lot of chains," Owen said bleakly, "and he still had that awful muzzle on. The guards were pretty much ignoring him. I managed to catch his eye, so he knows we're here."

"I don't know how we're going to free him," fretted Ivy, "with the guards right there."

Owen looked thoughtful for a moment. "Here's what we're

going to do," he said decisively. "I'm going to wheel the cart outside, like I'm going back for another load of eggs. What I'm really going to do is return to the forges for a hammer. There were tons of tools just lying around. If I'm careful, I think I can snatch one without being seen. If I can give the jaw piece of Elridge's muzzle a good bang or two, enough to loosen it, he'll be able to open his mouth to breathe fire."

"But the guards..." said Ivy.

"They're playing Knucklebones outside the door," Owen said, with a dismissive wave of his hand, "not paying attention at all. I should be able to sneak up unnoticed. By the time they hear me banging away, it'll be too late."

"What about the rest of Elridge's chains?" asked One-Oh-Three.

"Dragon fire is incredibly hot," said Owen. "He'll be able to melt those right off. He'll be able to melt the door to the vault, too, as big as it is." Owen's gaze drifted meaningfully toward the door. "That's how we're going to get the two of you out."

"Out?" One-Oh-Three's eyes widened. "You're going to leave us here?"

"Sure am," confirmed Owen. "You need to stay here and find the harp. But you'll have to be quick about it. If everything goes according to plan, you've probably only got about ten minutes or so before Elridge will be melting down that door. And once the guards realize what's going on, we're going to have to flee fast."

"We can follow the Steaming Stream to the exit that leads outside," One-Oh-Three said excitedly. "It lets out near the Kettle. You can drop me off and keep flying for Ardendale, harp in hand."

Ivy felt a huge rush of admiration for the stable boy. "Owen, you're brilliant!" she gushed.

"Well," said Owen, with an offhand shrug of his shoulders, "I guess for a stupid oaf and pinheaded simpleton, I'm not half bad." He turned to seize the cart handle.

"Owen—wait!" said Ivy, reaching out and grabbing his arm before he could walk away. "I don't care what Ninety-Seven or anyone else says. I think you're amazing. I would have never made it to the vault without you." She gave him a grateful smile, even as she felt her cheeks flush deeply. "I'm really glad you're here with me."

Owen turned red as a radish, but he looked immensely flattered.

"You'd better hurry and find that harp," he said, turning away shyly. "We don't have much time."

Owen banged on the door and was released by the guards. Ivy felt a stab of worry as she watched him go.

"Leaping lava, I had no idea the royal vault was so huge," said One-Oh-Three, looking a bit overwhelmed as he scanned the piles and piles of golden eggs. "Where do we even start looking?"

"Well, you take that side," Ivy gestured to her left, "and I'll start over here."

Trudging through the vault was not an easy undertaking. Eggs rolled beneath Ivy's feet, often sending her stumbling. She lost sight of One-Oh-Three as he disappeared behind a tall mound of eggs. After only a few minutes, the gleam from the massive quantities of gold started to hurt her eyes. At least the terrible, sulfurous smell was much less noticeable. Her nose must be growing accustomed to it.

Minutes soared by with no sign of the harp. Drenched in sweat from the stifling heat and frantic with worry, Ivy quickened her pace. Her legs went flying when an egg slipped from beneath her boot. She went tumbling in an avalanche of eggs, finally rolling to a stop at the bottom of one of the egg mountains.

"Ouch!" She rubbed her shin where the shadow of a bruise was already forming. "Oh, I'm going to be black and blue all over." Slowly, the princess staggered to her feet.

"Ivy!" came One-Oh-Three's shout from the other side of the vault. "Ivy, over here! I've found the harp!"

One-Oh-Three actually hadn't wandered far. Following the sound of his voice, it took her less than two minutes to find him among the mountains of eggs.

"Ivy, it's here!" The prince rushed up, wobbling on the unsteady footing. He grabbed her arm and pointed.

Nestled between two slopes was a solid gold pedestal. Perched on top was a beautiful golden harp, arched as elegantly as a swan's neck and topped with the bust of a handsome man with high cheekbones, a prominent nose, and eyes closed in slumber.

"I couldn't reach it," One-Oh-Three said, embarrassed.

Ivy hurried to the pedestal and, standing on tiptoes, managed to seize the golden harp by its base.

"Now let's get out of here," she said. But no sooner had the words left her mouth, than the strings of the harp began to strum of their own accord, releasing a long, discordant stream of babbling notes.

"What the—" Ivy glanced in shock at the instrument in her hands.

The harp's eyes flew open, and it let out a painfully loud cry that shook the air around them, echoing throughout the vault.

"THIEEEEEEEEEEEEEEF!"

Ivy winced at the sound, and One-Oh-Three covered his ears. The harp's cries were so piercing that she was sure the guards outside couldn't help but hear.

"THIEF! THIEF! THIEF!"

26

Fire Fight

"How do you shut this thing up?" Ivy shook the screaming harp, and when that didn't work, clapped her hand over its tiny mouth. Immediately, a sharp prick of pain spiked down her arm. "Ouch!" She jerked away. "The horrible thing just bit me," she said, disbelievingly, staring at the twin red crescents marring her palm.

There were noises on the other side of the door now, adding to the din inside the vault.

"Who's in there?" a gruff voice demanded. "I command you to surrender, in the name of the king!"

"THIEF! THIEF!" The harp continued to cry and pluck its strings.

"Fairy cakes," groaned Ivy. "I don't think Owen has had time to free Elridge yet."

The locks on the door began to unbolt, and the princess's heart leaped into her throat.

One-Oh-Three's face was white as he anxiously scanned their surroundings. "Quick! We have to hide!"

"They'll be able to hear us wherever we go," Ivy pointed out, gesturing to the screaming harp.

"Get rid of it," said One-Oh-Three. "We can come back for it later."

"I can't," said Ivy, miserably. She had been through so much to get the harp that she couldn't bear to risk losing it now.

"Then just run," cried the young prince, as the door to the vault wrenched open and five gold-armored guards burst inside. Ivy had time to catch a brief glimpse of their grim faces—they weren't wearing their helmets in the stifling heat. One-Oh-Three set off at a run, dashing behind the nearest bank of golden eggs. The princess followed. Beneath her arm, the golden harp continued to shriek.

"No one steals from the king of Jackopia!" cried the harp.

Ivy heard the clang of gold on gold as the guards gave chase. She couldn't imagine that running in golden armor over golden eggs was an easy task. She was having trouble keeping her own footing.

"Keep going, One-Oh-Three," she urged. "We need to stay ahead of them."

One-Oh-Three wove around mounds of eggs like a rabbit fleeing a fox, his small size making him quick and nimble. Ivy was hard-pressed to keep up. She tailed the prince around a bend—and nearly collided with him as he skidded to a stop.

"Dead end!" he cried.

They were surrounded on three sides by towering mountains of eggs, the slopes too steep to climb.

"Quick! Back the way we came!"

But it was too late. The guards, undoubtedly following the angry cries of the harp, had caught up, blocking Ivy and One-Oh-Three's only route of escape. The guards' swords were drawn, the golden blades glinting in the light.

"Now we have you," said the guard in the lead. Ivy realized who he was in the same instance recognition dawned on his own face. The stalwart Captain of the Guard was staring at her openmouthed, his expression a mixture of astonishment and dismay. "You? Here? In the royal vault? Oh, the king will not be pleased about this, not pleased at all." His gaze drifted past her, eyes rounding with surprise as they alighted on the young prince. "Your Highness?"

"Um, hello, Brom," said One-Oh-Three, giving an innocent little wave.

"What? How—" He turned on the guards behind him, his temper exploding. "Imbeciles! How could you let this happen? This is an inexcusable breach of security. You know the crown prince is not to be left unattended, let alone wandering in the royal vault. You'll be lucky if the king doesn't have you flayed for this." He squared his shoulders importantly. "It's a good thing I came on my rounds when I did. Come, Your Highness, we must return you to your chambers at once."

One-Oh-Three took a tentative step backward. "But Brom—"

An enormous crash at the front of the vault cut the prince's protest short. Ivy was nearly knocked from her feet as golden eggs came tumbling down around them. A long, reptilian face appeared over the top of one of the mounds, enshrouded by a golden helmet with a rather loose-looking jaw. Bits of melted chain dangled from both the helmet and the armor along his back.

"Elridge!" cried Ivy, happiness and relief rushing through her.

"Sorry we're late," said Owen, who was clinging to a spine atop the dragon's back, a hammer still grasped in one hand.

"The beast has escaped! Protect the prince!" ordered the Captain of the Guard, "and the king's treasure!" He wheeled so that One-Oh-Three was at his back. "Stay behind us, Your Highness. We won't let anything happen to you." Then he signaled his men to advance.

"You know, I'm usually a pretty easygoing dragon," said Elridge with an edge to his voice. "But today I've been deceived, threatened, shackled in chains, dragged underground, and now you want to skewer me with swords on top of everything else." His eyes flashed dangerously, and curls of smoke were leaking from beneath his helmet. "I'm starting to get a little annoyed."

Ivy knew what the light burning behind Elridge's eyes meant: The dragon was about to breathe fire.

"Come on," she said, dragging One-Oh-Three a safe distance away.

"Charge!" cried the Captain of the Guard, and five armored bodies rushed the dragon with their swords aloft.

Elridge let loose a stream of fire at their feet. Ivy never failed to be amazed by dragon fire, no matter how many times she saw it. Orange flames roared across the expanse of eggs, so intense that Ivy and One-Oh-Three turned their faces from the heat.

"Stand your ground, men!" shouted the captain.

But there was a series of yelps, and a clatter that sounded

suspiciously like the fleeing of armored feet. Ivy cautiously peered over her shoulder. The captain was bracing himself against the onslaught of flame just inches from his toes. He was quite alone.

"Weaklings!" he shouted, raising his voice so that the sound carried across the vault. "Am I the only man with a shred of courage around—*yeow!*" Armor clanking, he started hopping from one foot to the other. It took Ivy a moment to realize that the armor encasing his feet must be getting very hot, even if it wasn't directly in Elridge's line of fire. Heat was spreading rapidly; the golden eggs beneath Elridge's blaze were starting to glow red-orange.

The captain tried to back away, but Elridge redirected his column of flame, making sure it remained at the captain's feet.

"Ouch, ouch, ouch!" The armor-encased man continued to hop as if performing an enthusiastic, if somewhat inelegant, dance.

"Look at the golden eggs," gasped One-Oh-Three. "They're melting!"

Sure enough, eggs were dissolving beneath Elridge's fiery breath, a large golden puddle spilling out across the floor.

Owen was waving for their attention.

"Climb abroad!" he called, and Ivy and One-Oh-Three made quick work of clambering onto the dragon's back.

"Elridge, it's time to get out of here!" yelled Ivy, settling herself between two spines.

Elridge, who looked as if he was rather enjoying making the captain dance, cut his stream of fire with great reluctance.

"What, so soon?" he asked, disappointed.

"Elridge!"

"All right, I'm going, I'm going," huffed the dragon, swinging toward the entrance of the vault. "No need to get prickly about it."

"Not so fast, foul monster." The Captain of the Guard was scrambling up the side of an egg mountain. "I demand that you release the crown prince immediately!"

Before Ivy knew what was happening, the captain had launched himself at the unsuspecting dragon. He managed to seize one of the chains hanging from Elridge's battered helmet and dangled beneath the dragon's chin, brandishing his sword with his free hand.

"You're not taking the prince anywhere!" he cried. "I'll run you through if I have to!"

Elridge's scales kept him well-protected, but Ivy knew his head was one of his few areas of vulnerability. A sword that pierced the roof of his mouth could cut through to his brain. And faced with a sword mere handbreadths from his jaw, the dragon grew a little frantic.

"Get off me!" he shouted, shaking his head furiously from side to side, desperate to dislodge his unwelcome passenger.

The captain was flung about violently but managed to keep his grip. Ivy clung tightly to spine in front of her and tightened her grasp on the harp. If Elridge kept up such turbulent tossing, he might well shake his riders from their seats.

"Elridge, be careful!" she cried.

"If any harm befalls the prince, nothing will save you from my wrath!" The captain was swinging too wildly to get a clear thrust with his sword, but that didn't stop him from waving it menacingly. This spooked Elridge all the more. Still shaking his head, the dragon let loose another stream of fire, twice as large and intense as before. The brunt of it struck the mountain of eggs directly in front of him.

Fire was raging over the captain's head, but still the stubborn man hung on.

"Brom!" shouted One-Oh-Three. "I'm not in any danger. Let go!"

"Neverrrrrrrr!" The Captain of the Guard was being thrown about as if he was a collection of rags.

The mountain of eggs before Elridge was shrinking. Hot streams of gold flowed down its sides, flooding the floor of the vault, melting the eggs there as well.

"Elridge, you have to stop," pleaded Ivy. Her teeth rattled, and she felt like she was clinging to the back of a bucking horse. "You're going to destroy the vault!"

But the dragon was panicked beyond reason. Even the harp seemed cowed by the wild spray of dragon fire. Eyes closing, it fell silent for the first time since Ivy had snatched it from the pedestal.

Heat was spreading rapidly. The mound in front of Elridge was almost completely melted, and others were quickly following.

The Captain of the Guard eyed the steaming pool of gold beneath him. It was rising quickly. Knuckles tightening on the chain, he forced himself to look away. Ivy wasn't sure how much longer he could hold on. She was sure the chain, too, was growing very hot.

"Drop your sword!" she shouted at him.

"What?" The captain looked puzzled.

"Drop your sword! Elridge is scared you're going to stab him."

"Why should I?" demanded the captain.

"Because we're all going to cook if you don't!"

Elridge's legs were already completely submersed; molten gold was beginning to brush the dragon's belly. This didn't bother the scaled dragon, of course, but the rest of them would not hold up so well.

The Captain of the Guard looked uncertain.

"You said you wouldn't let anything happen to me," One-Oh-Three said beseechingly.

The captain hesitated only a second more before flinging his sword into the distance.

Elridge must have caught the winking of it in the light. He cut his billow of flame to watch the sword arch through the air. It landed with a splash and sank beneath the liquid gold.

"Yes, that's right," the captain snapped disagreeably. "I've gotten rid of the blasted blade. You can stop trying to churn me like butter."

The dragon's head gave one last, little twitch.

"You were going to stab me," he said accusingly, his voice feeble and shaken.

"You were trying to kidnap the crown prince," retorted the captain.

"Can we argue about this later?" Ivy's voice cracked, fear and exasperation getting the better of her. "If we don't get out of here fast, we're going to be boiled alive!"

27

Riding the Golden Tide

The pool of gold was swiftly rising. The golden statues, the chests of gems, the tall-masted ship—all had melted beneath its scalding surface. The remaining mounds of eggs were shrinking rapidly. Ivy now had a clear view of the door to the vault, which had been knocked askew when Elridge had burst through. It lay on its side across the opening, trapping the liquid gold like a beaver's dam. But it, too, was melting, and it was only a matter of time before it dissolved completely.

"Oh dear." Elridge took in the grim scene with horror. "I-I think I may have gotten a little carried away."

"A little carried away?" The captain's voice rose to a pitch of which Ivy would not have imagined the burly man capable. "A little carried away? You've ruined the king's treasure and destroyed a countless number of golden eggs!"

This seemed the wrong moment to point out that the royal

egg-countants *had* actually counted the number of eggs in the vault.

"Elridge, we have the harp," Ivy said instead. "Now you have to get us out of here. Everyone in Ardendale is counting on us."

Her words seemed to snap the dragon from his daze. It was a good thing, too. Liquid gold was closing in on the princess's toes. She could feel the scorching heat through the soles of her boots and drew her knees higher to buy herself a few more inches.

"I guess you're going to have to hop on for the ride," the dragon told the Captain of the Guard, who was still dangling from the chain beneath his chin. "Grab hold."

Before the captain could object, Elridge tossed his head, much the way Ivy had seen Ninety-Seven toss her hair. The captain went flying on the end of his chain, making a wide semicircle around the dragon's head. He collided none too gently with one of the spines on Elridge's back but had the wherewithal to grab hold, hauling himself into a sitting position behind Ivy.

"I don't know about this," he said doubtfully, wrapping his arms around the spine awkwardly. "I think I'd rather take my chances with the boiling gold."

"Doesn't it hurt?" One-Oh-Three asked Elridge. The prince's spectacles kept fogging over in the heat; he had to wipe the lenses with his sleeve so he could see.

"I breathe fire from my belly." Elridge shrugged. "A little melted gold's not going to hurt me."

"But can you move?" asked Ivy. The gold looked thick and gooey.

"It's a little sticky," said Elridge, "but I think I can manage. Watch your toes." He settled himself on top of the fiery-hot liquid, floating much like a duck on a pond. Paddling his legs, he propelled them toward the entrance to the vault.

"Actually, this isn't bad at all," said the dragon, sounding pleased. "I think we're in for smooth sailing."

Unfortunately, as he said this, Elridge was passing a half-melted mountain of eggs, which chose that moment to collapse. Ivy watched, horrified, as it came crashing down like the face of a cliff crumbling into the sea, sending up a tidal wave of molten gold. Ivy heard a scream escape her throat as Elridge and his passengers were lifted high into the air. Hot pricks of pain rained down on her face and arms as they were showered with burning drops of gold.

The stone overhang above the vault's entrance was rushing toward them at impossible speed and the ceiling of the cavern was directly overhead, leaving Elridge no room for flight. Ivy braced herself for a jarring impact. But suddenly there was a blur of rock before her eyes and the cries of her friends echoing in her ears.

They plummeted with the wave, bearing down on the broken door blocking the entrance. Only a thin layer of it had yet to melt. Elridge, moving too quickly to stop, smashed straight through, and liquid gold spilled into the space beyond.

The golden tide overshot the path outside the vault, surging into the Steaming Stream on the other side. Elridge was swept away by yet another searing flow.

In front of her, Ivy could see One-Oh-Three's shoulders shaking as he released a series of hiccuplike sounds. She thought the young prince was crying. It took a moment to realize that he was actually laughing—and quite gleefully at that.

"That was stupendous!" he cried. "I wish we could do it again!"

"No thank you," said the Captain of the Guard, sounding hoarse and out of breath.

"Oh dear, oh dear." Elridge was paddling frantically against the fast-moving stream. "This is no good—the current's too strong!"

"It's all right, Elridge," One-Oh-Three said, reassuringly. "Let the stream carry you. It'll take us to the surface, up to the lake."

This news calmed the dragon, who relaxed and let the stream sweep him along. Steam rose about them like a wispy fog, and Ivy had to mop her forehead so sweat didn't run into her eyes. She was grateful for her perch atop Elridge's back, above the boiling liquid. Beneath them, the stream ran amber, mixed with melted gold.

It's kind of pretty, thought the princess.

"Look—over there!" Owen's shout broke into her thoughts.

She lifted her gaze to see a small opening in the cave wall ahead, through which peeked a patch of blue sky. It grew larger and larger, and suddenly they were sailing through. Sunlight stung her eyes, and they spilled onto the surface of the simmering lake outside the city.

Elridge spread his wings and gave a tremendous flap. He barely lifted off the lake before plopping down heavily. "Good goat fur, this gold armor's too heavy," moaned the dragon. "It wasn't meant for flying, you know." The lower edges of his armor had melted a bit, but most of it was still intact.

"Can you swim to shore?" Ivy asked. "Then we'll get the armor off so you can fly us home."

"Not so fast," growled the Captain of the Guard. "You can't run off with the king's harp. *And* you have to answer for what you've done to the royal treasure."

A clamor of voices made the princess turn toward shore. She was dismayed to see a large crowd of people gathering at the water's edge: a number of gold-armored guards flanked the king, the queen, Ninety-Seven, Ninety-Eight, Master Puckle, and a handful of attendants. Once again, the guards had their swords drawn. The king was glaring at the group on the lake, his face as rigid as granite, his mouth drawn into a tight, grim line.

"His Majesty appears to agree," said the captain, satisfaction in his voice.

One-Oh-Three glanced over his shoulder at Ivy, pale-faced.

The princess stared at the harp still clutched in her hand, her heart sinking like a stone. They had been so close.

28

A Monarch's Day Surprise

"**W**e left the castle with a contingent of guards this morning," said the king. "Even your mother was well enough to come along. She's felt much better since I assured her you would be watched at all times. It was early, before breakfast, but I was eager to start my inspection of the city with the royal architects. The sooner we finished, the sooner we could hold the feast."

One-Oh-Three groaned. "It's Monarch's Day," he whispered to Ivy. "I'd forgotten."

"There was no need for you to arise at such an hour, One-Oh-Three, so we decided to let you sleep," continued the king. "Then, only minutes ago, we were met by a guard from the castle. He could barely breathe, as he had run the entire way; but he managed to convey that the Crown Prince had been spotted inside the royal vault and was in danger of being roasted by the dragon, who had escaped its bonds."

Laying a hand to her forehead, the queen gave a piteous

moan. Two servants were holding her upright, and five more fanned her.

The king was pacing as he had before, back and forth, wearing a furrow in the dry soil alongside the lake. Ivy, Owen, and One-Oh-Three stood before him like prisoners awaiting a sentence while Elridge—surrounded by nearly a dozen guards with swords at the ready—looked on helplessly.

There was quite a crowd of spectators. In addition to the group from the castle, the excitement had drawn a fair number of onlookers from the city. Ninety-Seven and Ninety-Eight looked particularly delighted to see Ivy in so much trouble. Master Puckle probably would have, as well, except that his own young charge was caught up in the mess.

"We were rushing back to the castle when we saw you burst out onto the lake," said the king.

"Oh, my p-poor, poor One-Oh-Three," cried the queen. "He could have f-f-fallen in the w-w-water."

"The good captain tells me that not only did you endanger the life of my son a second time, but you attempted to steal a national treasure and destroyed the entire contents of the royal vault in the process!" The king paused midstep and took several deep breaths, but apparently could not contain the rage building within him. In a display that Largessa would have been proud of, his face turned three shades of deepening red and a thunderous bellow burst forth.

"HOW COULD YOU?" he roared at Ivy. "There isn't a single golden egg left—not a single one! You melted the entire vault! All that precious gold—wasted, ruined forever. Such unthinkable treachery, after I took you into my own castle. This is beyond an act of treason! This is an act of war!" The king's eyes were wild, the whites unnaturally bright against the red of his skin. "If that giantess doesn't crush your wicked little kingdom, rest assured I'm going to raise an army that will!"

"Father," One-Oh-Three broke in anxiously. "Please, you can't blame Ivy. This is my fault. She was only helping me."

Ivy was as startled by this as the king.

"Helping *you?*" he scoffed. "A likely story! This pilfering princess seems to have corrupted you to the core, One-Oh-Three. Now she has you lying for her. What, did you just happen to think you needed help melting all the eggs in the royal vault?"

"Yes, that's exactly what happened," One-Oh-Three answered plainly. "It was a surprise for you, for Monarch's Day."

The king sputtered indignantly. "This? This is your idea of a surprise?"

"I wanted to give you something special," explained his son, "a golden marvel that no other kingdom could boast."

"A bunch of melted eggs?" the king asked crossly.

"No." One-Oh-Three swept out his palm, gesturing behind him. "A lake of gold."

The king was speechless. Ivy herself had no words as she turned with the crowd to behold what everyone besides One-Oh-Three had failed to notice. The Kettle was golden, the entire lake colored by the melted eggs that had flowed down the Steaming Stream from the vault.

The king struggled to speak, but it was several moments before he found his voice again. "A lake of gold?" The ghost of a smile touched his lips.

"I couldn't tell you ahead of time because it would have

spoiled the surprise," said One-Oh-Three, giving Ivy a sly wink. "I figured you wouldn't mind us using the gold in the royal vault. After all, the hens lay so quickly, it'll be full again in no time."

"Yes, very true, full again in no time," echoed the king, who was still staring at the Kettle in awe.

"I hope you like it, Father," One-Oh-Three said, tentatively.

"Like it?" The king's face lit up like a child being presented with a puppy, and he was openly smiling now. "Like it? Why, I love it! I can't believe I have my very own lake of gold. Oh, the other kingdoms will be so jealous." He slipped an arm over his son's scrawny shoulders. "One-Oh-Three, you clever boy, you've made this the best Monarch's Day ever."

One-Oh-Three looked pleased by the praise. "It meant I had to leave the castle."

The king studied his son thoughtfully. "Perhaps we *have* been a little too strict with you," he admitted, readily. "You might be small for your age, but it's quite clear that you have a good head on your shoulders. After all, any young prince who can accomplish this"—the king made a sweeping gesture to the golden lake—"is certainly capable enough to leave the castle from time to time."

"What!" cried the queen, shocked.

"Now, Hortensia, I know you worry, but we must let him grow up sometime," said her husband.

"But not yet!" insisted the queen, flapping her handkerchief feverishly. "He's still far too small."

But this time, the king was not swayed by her words. "One day, One-Oh-Three will be ruler of this fine kingdom. We can hardly keep treating him as if he were a baby." The king gave his wife a gentle smile. "Hortensia, you know I would never allow it unless I thought it safe. I love the boy as much as you do, my dear."

The queen slowly stopped fanning herself. "Well," she said, hesitantly, looking between her husband and son, "I suppose if your father thinks it safe...we can arrange for some carefully supervised outings—with a healer on hand and a large contingent of armed guards." She wiped her tears and took a long sip from the golden goblet handed to her by a servant. "I'll just have the royal apothecary brew larger quantities of calming draught."

One-Oh-Three beamed. "It's a start," he said happily.

The king squeezed One-Oh-Three's shoulders approvingly. "You're going to go down in the history books for this, my boy," he gushed. "Future generations of Jackopians will tell the story of how my very own son created a magnificent golden lake— and all for his beloved father."

"Well," One-Oh-Three said nonchalantly, "I had help. I never would have managed to get into the royal vault or melt the golden eggs if it wasn't for Ivy, Owen, and Elridge."

"Oh yes, well, then I suppose I should thank them as well," said the king, who was so distracted by the shimmering lake that he didn't actually thank them at all.

"I was sure you would feel that way," said One-Oh-Three. "That's why I gave Ivy the golden harp, as a thank-you for their help. I knew you wouldn't mind. It's not like we ever use it, anyway. It's a rather small price to pay for an entire lake of gold, don't you think?"

"I suppose," said the king, waving a ring-encrusted hand as if he had more important matters that needed his attention.

"Yes, fine, let them take it." He turned to the attendants closest to him. "Forget the rest of my royal inspection. Fetch some tables and tell everyone to bring food at once. I want to have my Monarch's Day feast now, right here, on the shores of my stunning new golden lake."

29

Ardendale Under Siege

"Thanks for getting your father's guards to remove Elridge's armor," Ivy said to One-Oh-Three, as they sat waiting for the dragon to be freed from what remained of his golden casing.

"I'm sorry it's taking so long," said the prince. "The armor was a bit battered and it's not coming off as easily as it should. They're having to crack open parts of it." He glanced over at Elridge, who had nearly a dozen guards—plus Owen—banging on his armor with hammers from the royal forges.

A short distance away, the king and company celebrated on the shores of the golden lake. There were tables laden with food and sweets, but Ivy found that she didn't have much of an appetite. Instead, she sat on a boulder by the water, fidgeting impatiently with the golden harp. Tomorrow was Largessa's deadline. They needed to get home fast.

"I told them to hurry," said One-Oh-Three, as if he hoped

this would bolster her mood. "I know you have to get back to Ardendale as soon as possible."

"I guess I'm just a little nervous about making it on time," said Ivy. "Thank you for all you've done, One-Oh-Three. That was genius, what you said about the golden lake and how you got the king to give us the harp. You're so knowledgeable and clever—and you've got a good heart. I can tell you're going to make a great ruler."

"You will, too," said One-Oh-Three.

"Me?" she snorted. "The only thing I'm great at is shirking responsibility. I don't think I have what it takes to be a leader."

"That's not true," protested One-Oh-Three. "Look at all you've done: crossing the Speckled Sea, plotting to steal the harp, sneaking into the royal vault, risking my father's wrath. Anyone who would go to such lengths to save her kingdom obviously cares about her people. You're brave and kind, Ivy. You're going to be a better ruler than you think."

"I hope so," said the princess, a fierce new determination settling in her chest. "One thing's for certain: I'm going to try a lot harder from now on."

"I'm glad," said the prince, "and I'm glad you came to Jackopia. I would have never gotten to ride a dragon if you hadn't. And I'd still be confined to the castle. I've never had a friend before," he said sadly. "I'm going to miss you once you're gone."

"We'll see each other again," Ivy said confidently. "You can come visit me in Ardendale. Elridge and I will fly you over—your guards, too, if your mother insists on having them along. We can show you the Fringed Forest and the Smoke Sand Hills, where the dragons live. It'll be a lot of fun." Her mood fell sharply again. "That is, if everything doesn't get crushed by falling rocks."

"It won't," One-Oh-Three said earnestly. "You're going to get there in time. You just *have* to!"

They sat in silence for a few minutes as the guards continued to pound on Elridge's armor.

"You know," said One-Oh-Three, looking proud, "people are saying my golden lake is a feat worthy of Jack the Brave, Mighty, and Truly Magnificent."

Ivy gave him a warm smile. "Don't tell anyone I said this, but I think it's far, far worthier."

"Ivy, we're ready!" Owen called, jogging to her, with a hammer still in hand.

The princess saw her dragon friend was indeed finally gold-free. He was arching his back and stretching his wings, glad to be relieved of the burden.

"I say good riddance to the lot of you," came a snooty voice.

Ivy glanced up to see Ninety-Seven and Ninety-Eight approaching on their dainty golden slippers.

"Now we won't have to share lessons with a pathetic princess from some backwater hole," said Ninety-Seven, shooting a nasty glance at Ivy, "or put up with her fumbling help." Her haughty gaze shifted to Owen, who dropped his eyes to the ground. "How sad, that there isn't even enough gold in Ardendale to hire a decent servant," she said with a sniff.

Ivy saw the shame on Owen's face, and something inside her snapped.

"Owen is courageous and kind and loyal," she said fiercely, linking her arm through the stable boy's. "And he isn't a servant, he's my friend. But you wouldn't understand such things, Ninety-Seven, seeing as all the gold in Jackopia couldn't buy the likes of you one of those."

Ivy gave Owen her biggest smile and guided him toward Elridge, leaving Ninety-Seven openmouthed, sputtering indignantly.

Ivy settled onto Elridge's back, with Owen behind, and secured both herself and the harp with the rope they had brought from Ardendale.

"Here we go," said Elridge, lifting off with a great whoosh of his wings.

"Good-bye, Ivy!" called One-Oh-Three, waving fervently as his friends took to the air. "Good luck!"

The night over the Speckled Sea was a rough one. A fierce storm blew in from the north, forcing Elridge to fly against the wind. Several times, the lightning grew so intense that the dragon had to set down on the water, unable to resume until it passed. Between the thunder, pelting rain, and gnawing worry, Ivy got little in the way of sleep.

Adding to her apprehension was her inability to contact anyone in Ardendale. Throughout the evening and late into the night, she tried several times to use Drusilla's magic mirror. Whatever room she asked to see—her father's bedchamber, Drusilla's bedchamber, the Great Hall, Tildy's sitting room, even Rose and Clarinda's tiny chambers in the servant's wing of the castle—was dark and empty. She was filled with a terrible foreboding.

"They've headed to safety, that's all," Owen said reassuringly.

"Remember the plan was to evacuate before Largessa started flinging rocks. I'm sure they're all fine."

Ivy had hoped they would make good time, but the storm raged late into the night, clearing only a few hours before daybreak. It was well after dawn by the time a thin sliver of land appeared on the horizon. Even from this distance, the princess could see the meanstalk, a huge column of green twisting up into the clouds.

"Can you go any faster?" Ivy hated to ask, as she was sure Elridge was weary from flying through the night, but the situation was desperately urgent.

"I'll... try," panted the dragon.

"Do you see that?" exclaimed Owen, pointing toward the distant shore. "Oh no, that can't be good."

Ivy could make out the castle now, perched on a rise next to the sea. Black masses were raining from the sky, near the top of the meanstalk, and she could hear thunderous crashes as they collided with the castle's stone walls.

"Largessa's attacking the kingdom!" Her heart gave a leap so immense she feared it might burst through her chest. "Hurry, Elridge—fly!"

The dragon heaved a deep breath and flapped his wings for all he was worth. They shot through the air like a dart, the sea a blur beneath them. The rush of wind made Ivy's eyes water. She squinted and saw the castle fast approaching through her narrowed lids.

The garden was littered with black boulders as well as debris from the damage to the castle. A boulder sat in a gaping hole in the center of the walk above the castle gate, and the roof of the gatehouse had collapsed entirely. There wasn't much left of the small southern tower; Ivy could see into the little room at the top, where half the wall was missing.

"She's destroying the castle!" cried the princess.

"Look, over by the old mill!"

Ivy tore her eyes from the devastation, directing her attention to where Owen pointed. The miller's field was opposite the castle gate, across the Inland Road. Ivy spotted a familiar white-bearded figure near the line of trees bordering the field, waving frantically.

"Father!" she shouted.

Elridge had spotted the king, as well. He made a beeline for the field, setting down in the long grass.

Her father rushed forward to meet them, and Ivy could see now that he was not alone. Drusilla, Boggs, Tildy, and a handful of the King's Guard came pouring from the cellar door of the miller's cottage, hurrying out to join them.

"What are you doing here?" Ivy called to her father, raising her voice to carry over the noise. Across the road, another black boulder slammed into the castle. "I thought you were going to head north for safety."

"The people have gone," said the king, "escorted by the King's Guard. Only a few of us remained behind to wait for you, Ivy. When Largessa finishes crushing the castle, she will undoubtedly try to destroy the rest of the kingdom. We thought it safest to hide underground in the miller's cellar. You have brought the harp, haven't you?" His eyes searched for it hopefully.

"It's right here," said Ivy, gesturing to the golden instrument in front of her, strapped to Elridge's spine.

"You must take it to Largessa," said the king, "and I fear that won't be easy, with those rocks raining down like mad. Elridge, my friend, do you think you're up for the flight?"

Ivy knew the journey across the sea had taken its toll. Elridge looked very tired.

"I'll try," he said without hesitation, and Ivy was touched by his courage.

"I'm coming, too," said Drusilla, pushing to the front of the crowd.

Her face was tight and angry, which was unusual for the sweet-natured fairy, but Ivy had to admit that her godmother seemed much more composed than the last time the princess had seen her. Not so much as the hint of a hiccup marred her speech.

"Drusy, love, is that such a good idea—" began Boggs.

"Of course it is," Drusilla cut in sharply. "I'm through standing by and doing nothing while my home and my darling Toadstool are in harm's way. This is all my fault, and it's about time I see things set right—*before* the castle is smashed to smithereens."

She looked around defiantly, as if daring someone to argue with her. This time, no one did.

"Owen, jump down quickly," she commanded. "I'm taking your seat."

30

Confrontations

As last time, the stalk disappeared into the clouds, making for a harrowing flight, for it was difficult to see the falling boulders until they were nearly upon the speeding dragon. With his sharp dragon eyesight, Elridge usually had time to dodge before they hit. There were a couple of close calls, however, and Ivy cringed every time she felt the rush of air as a boulder tore by.

"You seem better," she said to her godmother, more as a distraction from the perilous situation than anything else.

"Yes, I've had time to calm down a bit over the last several days," said Drusilla, ducking her head as another boulder shot past, "and to think things through. You were right to be upset with me, Ivy. It was terrible of me to leave Largessa in such a state, even if it wasn't intentional, and I'm going to do everything I can to make sure this situation is put to rights—starting now." She began to flap one hand back and forth in front of her, as if she were gesturing for someone to move out of the way.

Ivy was amazed to see the clouds part before them, blown aside by some unseen wind. But she shouldn't have been surprised. Drusilla had always had a knack for tinkering with the weather.

"Drusilla...that's...fantastic," huffed an out-of-breath Elridge. "Keep...it...up."

He swerved around the next two boulders, but Ivy could see that his pace was starting to slow. She recalled how difficult it had been for him to fly up the stalk the first time—when he had been well rested and carried only a single passenger.

"Not much farther, Elridge," she said encouragingly. "You can make it."

"Hope...so," he wheezed in reply. At this point, only sheer determination seemed to be keeping him in the air.

He gave two more flaps of his scalloped wings, the effort so great that he seemed not to notice the large black boulder hurtling toward them.

"Elridge, look out!" she cried.

At the last moment, the dragon banked steeply to one side, but even Ivy hadn't seen the second boulder, falling closely on the tail of the first. In evading one, Elridge had put himself directly in the path of the other. He flapped furiously, trying to clear the second boulder, but it glanced off his left wing, sending the dragon spiraling out of control. For several seconds, the world was a blur of blue sky and green leaves as he reeled toward the towering meanstalk.

Ivy's heart lurched.

Not the meanstalk! That thing will eat us alive!

In the seconds before impact, she thought she felt an odd tingling sensation, making the hairs on her arms rise. Perhaps it was just sheer terror. Then, claws stretched outward, Elridge crashed into the stalk amidst a cluster of heart-shaped leaves. The dragon immediately started to thrash and scream, and Ivy panicked, sure that pods were sinking their hungry teeth into his scaled flesh.

Drusilla seemed strangely unperturbed. "Oh, honestly, Elridge, stop making such a fuss," she said.

Puzzled, Ivy peered over the dragon's side. Up and down the meanstalk, pods were splitting open as before. This time, however, there wasn't a single snapping jaw in sight. The pods were opening to reveal enormous sweet-smelling white flowers— hundreds and hundreds of them, all along the stalk as far as the eye could see.

Ivy gaped at her godmother in astonishment.

Drusilla giggled deviously, looking immensely pleased with herself. "Much better, if I do say so myself."

Elridge had finally recognized that he wasn't in immediate danger.

"D-d-drusy?" He, too, stared at Drusilla, greatly impressed. "You saved us."

"My magic may be rather limited," said the fairy, smiling smugly, "but I have always, *always* been great at conjuring flowers." She sobered and peered at the dragon with concern. "How's your wing? Can you still get us to the top of the stalk?"

"It's a bit sore," confessed Elridge, flexing it tenderly. "But there's nothing wrong with my claws. Without those pods trying to make a meal of me, I can climb this thing easily."

He seized the leafy trunk and hauled himself higher, claw over claw. Before long, the gray stone of the cloud cliffs came into view.

"Largessa, please, let's talk about this." The desperate voice belonged to Gizzle the Green.

"I'm through talking," came an angry reply. "Now it's time for my revenge." Another black boulder went plunging over the edge of the cliffs.

Elridge pulled himself over the ledge. Ivy could see that Largessa was still barefoot and in her nightdress. She was hurling rocks at the world below and enjoying herself immensely. She laughed wildly, her bloodshot eyes gleaming. Next to her was an enormous wheelbarrow and a huge pile of black boulders. She had hauled them herself, judging by the streaks of dirt on her arms and nightdress.

She could keep this up for hours, Ivy thought with despair, when she saw the size of the pile.

Gizzle leaned heavily against his staff as four young branches wrapped around his neck and shoulders, the grass beneath his feet stretching up to stroke his legs. Next to him was his vine-covered cart, bearing a familiar-looking gilded birdcage. Unlike the distracted giantess, the plant mage spotted them immediately.

"*Hedera helix*, you sure took your sweet time getting back here with that harp," he exclaimed huffily, thumping toward the cliff's edge to meet them. Largessa, still lobbing boulders and laughing madly, seemed not to have noticed that anybody else was even there. Then Gizzle froze in his tracks, eyes narrowing behind his shaggy fringe of hair.

"Drusilla, what in bleeding blossoms are *you* doing here?

Haven't you caused enough—" Gizzle stopped short as his eyes fell upon the huge white flowers now adorning the meanstalk. His jaw fell open, and he whirled on Drusilla, who had just alighted from Elridge's back. "What have you done to my meanstalk?" he demanded, his voice cracking, his expression equal parts anger and disbelief.

But Drusilla's attention was focused solely on one thing.

"Toadstool," she cried, rushing toward the birdcage—and the small, furry figure it contained.

"Drusy, I knew you'd come for me!" Toadstool pawed at the bars of her prison like a digging puppy. "You have no idea the horrors I've been through. Quick! Get me out of this thing."

Drusilla undid the lock and snatched up her pet in her arms. "Toadstool! I've missed you so much," she murmured, sounding close to tears as she buried her face in the goat's white fur. "I've been worried sick. I'm so glad you're okay."

"Thanks to me," snapped Gizzle. A branch was stroking his left cheek. Irritated, the plant mage jerked his head away. "Largessa wanted to feed her to the meanstalk first thing, but I talked her into saving the messiest part for last. Yes, your annoying little goat's fine—better than my meanstalk. Just look at it. Now it's even more useless than a magical marigold. Doesn't blow bubbles or anything. All that hard work, all those gnashing teeth, all that nasty bleeding completely gone to waste!"

"That thing was an eyesore," Drusilla said, clutching Toadstool to her chest, "and it would have eaten us. My flowers are a huge improvement."

"You're just like those mulch-brains at B.B.I.M.F.," Gizzle said accusingly. "You never did appreciate my work. In any case, you've got a lot of nerve, showing your face here after stealing Largessa's harp."

"I didn't steal that silly harp," retorted Drusilla, who sounded as if she was getting very tired of hearing that particular accusation. "Jack stole the harp. I was just trying to keep his dear mother from starving."

"Hah! You expect me to believe that? After you stole my magic beans? I know you never cared about me, Drusilla. It was the magic beans you wanted all along."

"That's not true!" protested Drusilla. "I never meant to hurt you, Gizzle. We just weren't right for each other. There's no need to be angry and bitter just because I ended our engagement."

"Bitter, am I?" Gizzle's voice rose in indignation. "Perhaps you'd be bitter, too, if you'd spent the last nine centuries alone and miserable after having your heart broken."

Their raised voices had finally caught Largessa's attention. She swung her head in their direction, eyes blazing like black beacons, as if she couldn't believe anyone would dare interrupt her fun.

"Um, Drusilla." While Drusilla and Gizzle had been arguing, the princess had climbed from Elridge's back, bringing the harp with her. Now she tugged fearfully at her godmother's sleeve. "Drusilla, we have company—*big* company."

Both Drusilla and Gizzle abruptly ceased their bickering. Largessa looked as angry as a bull about to charge.

"Oh, hello there, Largessa," Drusilla said in her friendliest voice, wriggling her fingers in a dainty wave. She was still holding Toadstool, who had started to quiver again. "It's lovely to meet you at last. I've heard lots of…nice…things about you."

Gizzle's laugh was a nervous titter. "Largessa, we have good news. Drusilla and her friends have brought you the harp!" He looked at the giantess hopefully. "Isn't that wonderful? Exactly what you've been waiting for all these centuries."

If Largessa was pleased, she had a strange way of showing it: She took aim and heaved a large black boulder straight at them.

31

Lullaby

Everyone scattered as the boulder hurtled through the air. Between his injured leg and the branches wrapping around his body, Gizzle didn't make it more than a few steps. He stumbled and toppled to the ground, taking Ivy with him. The boulder sailed harmlessly over their heads.

"Drusilla," growled Largessa, hefting another. "At last! I never thought I'd get the chance. I've dreamed of this moment—or would have, if I *could* dream. But no, you took that from me, as well." Her lips curved in a vicious snarl. "And now it's time for you to pay. How I will enjoy crushing you and everyone you hold dear."

Drusilla had scrambled to the far side of the cliff, Toadstool still cradled in her arms.

"Largessa, I can't tell you how sorry I am," she said with great sincerity. "I had no idea Jack would use those magic beans to steal from you or that you'd been sleepless all these centuries. This has all been a truly terrible misunderstanding."

"Misunderstanding?" The giantess's grip tightened on the boulder, her knuckles turning white. "You call the nightmare I've been living a 'misunderstanding'?"

"The nightmare is over," Drusilla said brightly. "We've brought the harp back to you. I know it doesn't make up for all you've suffered, but I hope it's a start."

Largessa's lips stretched thin and bloodless, stark against the red of her face. Then she exploded. "BLAST THAT YOU BROUGHT THE HARP BACK!" she raged. "DO YOU HAVE ANY IDEA WHAT YOU'VE PUT ME THROUGH? I'M GOING TO PULVERIZE YOUR FAIRY FLESH! AND SAY GOOD-BYE TO YOUR GOAT, YOUR GODDAUGHTER, YOUR ENTIRE KINGDOM. WHEN I GET THROUGH, THERE WILL BE NOTHING LEFT OF ANYTHING THAT MATTERS TO YOU!"

"Drusilla, look out!" Ivy cried as Largessa let the boulder fly.

With a little squeak from Toadstool, Drusilla dove to one side, escaping by inches. Enraged at having missed her target twice, Largessa kicked two of the giant boulders over the edge of the cliff and angrily seized a third.

"I'M GOING TO GRIND YOUR FAIRY BONES TO DUST IF IT'S THE LAST THING I DO!"

Ivy cringed, ears ringing with Largessa's bellowed threats, and clambered to her feet. "I don't understand," she said to Gizzle. "I thought Largessa wanted the harp back."

"She *does*." Gizzle was struggling to stand, but the clinging branches made it nearly impossible. "She's so exhausted and angry, she can't think straight anymore. All she can focus on now is revenge."

Ivy watched helplessly as her godmother dodged another flying boulder. "We have to help Drusilla!"

Elridge seemed to have had the same thought. Nostrils smoking, the dragon uttered a cry that sounded more strangled than fierce and charged as Largessa bent to seize another boulder. The giantess easily sidestepped Elridge's clumsy attack, grabbing the end of his tail as he shot past. She gave it a yank so forceful, the dragon was jerked off his feet. He landed heavily on his belly, expelling a loud *oomph*, as the air was knocked from his lungs—and, it seemed, the fire as well. Two puffs of smoke mushroomed from his nostrils, then no more.

"Largessa, please," pleaded Drusilla. "This is all my fault. No one else needs to get hurt."

"This *is* all your fault," sneered Largessa, tossing aside Elridge's tail. Freed of her grasp, the dragon scuttled away like a fleeing crab. "And others *will* get hurt, but that's on *your* head, fairy, not mine. First thing's first: I'm going to finish what I've started and crush your kingdom to pieces." She once again reached toward the pile of black boulders.

"Do something!" Seizing Gizzle's arm, Ivy hauled the fumbling plant mage to his feet, rather roughly. "Can't you reason with her?"

"What do you think I've been trying to do for the past week?" snapped Gizzle. "She's gone mad from the lack of sleep. She won't listen to anyone or anything at this point, unless..." His eyes settled on the golden harp at their feet, where it had tumbled from Ivy's grasp when she'd fallen. Gingerly, he stooped to retrieve it.

"How do you work this thing?" He began plucking desperately at the strings.

"I don't know," said Ivy. "Isn't it supposed to play itself?" The only time she had heard the harp make any kind of sound was when she had stolen it from the royal vault. She cringed at the memory.

"Of course," said Gizzle. "So play, you stupid thing." He shook the harp as if he hoped this would stir it to life. "Play! Play!"

Ivy didn't think a shouted command would be enough to rouse the harp, but she was wrong. The harp promptly opened its eyes, and with a ripple of notes, began to play.

Music quivered in the air. Ivy had to admit it was extraordinarily beautiful, as flawless and golden as the instrument that produced it. Largessa had lifted another boulder high over her head, intent on flinging it at the world below. But now she paused, recognition flickering across her face, and something about her seemed to change.

"I know that song," she said, her face softening. Slowly, she lowered her arms. "It's my favorite. The one you used to play for me every night." She turned to stare at the harp in Gizzle's hand, amazement etched across her haggard features. "You remember. After all these years, you still remember."

She took a small step toward Gizzle, then another, the boulder falling from her hands, the beginnings of a smile blossoming on her lips. "I'd almost forgotten how lovely it sounds, how nice it makes me feel. So warm and...sleepy." Indeed, her eyelids were starting to droop, as if they had grown unbelievably heavy. She sank to her knees, too drowsy to even stay on her feet. "Bring the harp closer, Gizzle," she pleaded. "I want to hear every note."

The plant mage did as she asked. Hobbling with his staff, he limped forward and set the harp on the ground before her. She sighed contentedly, absorbed in the music.

"How I've missed you, my friend," she said, tears glistening on her cheeks as she reached out to stroke the harp's golden curves. "Your beautiful melodies always did have a way of soothing me."

Largessa struggled to keep her eyes open as sleep threatened to overcome her. "I'm sorry I've been so beastly," she said to those on the cliff top. "I'm not normally like this, you see, but I get a little cranky without sleep."

"You don't say," Elridge muttered under his breath. He swung his tail around to examine the tip, as if afraid Largessa had left a mark.

"Quite understandable," Drusilla said kindly. "You've been through a lot. I'm glad the harp is back where it belongs, and I hope you'll forgive any part I played in the wrongdoings against you. I can assure you it was quite unintentional."

"I've done wrong against you, as well," said Largessa, trying, without success, to stifle an enormous yawn. She laid down on her side and drew her knees to her chest, like a small child. "I would have crushed your kingdom. I've behaved monstrously."

"Well, I can forgive you if you can forgive me," said Drusilla, smiling.

Largessa smiled, too, before her sleepy-eyed gaze drifted to the plant mage. "You did it, Gizzle," she said, looking at him with open affection. "You got the harp back for me, just as you said you would. You didn't give up, and you didn't abandon me, even when I screamed and threw fits. You truly are the most kindhearted, wonderful man I've ever met."

This time, it was Gizzle's face that reddened, especially when she reached out and took his calloused hand in her enormous one.

"I don't know how much longer I can keep my eyes open," she said groggily. "You won't leave, will you? You'll still be here when I wake up?" Her voice was softer, more hopeful than Ivy would have imagined possible.

"Um, well, I suppose I could be," said Gizzle, looking surprised but also very pleased. "I mean, I was planning to go home to my greenhouse and feed my *Dionaea muscipula*, but . . . things never quite work out the way I plan." He squeezed her hand in return. "This would be nicer, anyway. The greenhouse can get a bit lonely, to tell the truth."

"Then I'll see you . . . when I wake," said the giantess. Her eyes drifted closed, but she didn't let go of Gizzle's hand.

The plant mage didn't look like he minded.

"Sweet dreams, Largessa," he said. "Sweet dreams."

Largessa fell asleep with a smile on her face.

A New Leaf

Elridge's wing was still a bit sore, so the flight down the meanstalk went very slowly. It helped, though, that the dragon could now perch on the stalk from time to time when he needed a rest. Drusilla didn't seem too concerned about how long the trip was taking; she spent the entire time cuddling with her "Toady-Woady" and telling the tiny pixie goat how much she had missed her. Ivy, on the other hand, fretted about the damage to the castle, of which she had a distressingly good view.

"Largessa may not have destroyed it," she said sadly, "but she came awfully close." Below them, the castle looked like the site of a great battle. Stone walls had been smashed, at least two of the towers had toppled, and black boulders were strewn about the courtyard and grounds.

"Cheer up, Ivy," said Drusilla, looking up from tickling Toadstool behind the ears. "Every castle worth its salt takes a good beating or two over the centuries. I've seen it over and over again. If a castle isn't ravaged by fire, then it's pummeled by catapults or besieged by armies. Castles are hardier than you'd imagine. Some mortar and a few new stones, and it'll be good as new."

"I hope so," said Ivy, who found it difficult to see her home in such a state.

Elridge made a gentle landing in the miller's meadow, across from what was left of the castle gate. The king, Tildy, Boggs, and Owen waited with the handful of the King's Guard.

"The boulders have stopped falling," said the king, rushing forward to meet Ivy as she slid from the dragon's back. "Has Largessa ended her attack? Is the kingdom saved?"

"Yes," said Ivy, laughing quite freely as she threw her arms around her father. "I don't think we'll have any more problems with Largessa—thanks to Drusilla. We never would have made it to the top of the meanstalk without her." The princess turned to face her fairy godmother, who had been greeting Boggs with hugs and kisses.

"Drusilla, I am so sorry for getting angry at you," she said. "What happened with Largessa was a long time ago, and I know you didn't mean for anyone to get hurt."

"No," said Drusilla, "you were right, Ivy. Fairies are rather thoughtless by nature, but that's no excuse. I made the decision to live in the human world, to serve as godmother to the princesses of Ardendale. I need to act with more responsibility."

"Me, too," admitted Ivy with a pang of guilt. "There's so much I don't know about ruling a kingdom, and so many people counting on me. Tildy, I promise to take my studies more seriously from now on."

"That is good news indeed," said Tildy with a smile.

"And, for what it's worth, I'm really, really glad to have you as my teacher," added the princess, thinking of the unpleasant Master Puckle. "I'll try to be more appreciative." The warm scent of lavender enveloped her as she leaned forward to wrap her arms around her nursemaid.

"Well," said Tildy, returning the hug with affection, "our kingdom should get pelted by giant boulders more often."

"I can help with Ivy's studies, too," offered Drusilla.

Tildy looked doubtful at this.

"I know I haven't always been a good influence in that regard," said Drusilla apologetically. "But I've never had a goddaughter who was heir to the throne before." The fairy beamed. "You've always been something special, Ivy, and I'll try to be a more conscientious godmother from now on. I need to encourage you in your studies rather than distract you from them."

"It *would* be nice, not always having you thwart my efforts," said Tildy.

"It sounds like you're both turning over a new leaf," the king said approvingly. "And just in time—we've a lot of work ahead of us. We must send word that it's safe for the people to return to their homes. We must see to the castle, as well. Repairing it is going to be quite the undertaking, I'm afraid." He turned to speak with his guards.

"It seems we're going to be rather busy," said Drusilla, slipping an arm around her goddaughter's shoulders. "But we can still have fun from time to time, can't we?"

"Of course," laughed Ivy.

"Speaking of fun," Drusilla said brightly, "I fixed your

bridesmaid's dress while you were away. Once my powers were under control again, it was easy to do. The flowers are as fresh and beautiful as ever. I even got the butterflies back. Now you can wear it again and again, for all sorts of occasions!"

Ivy's good mood suddenly sank, just a little. "Can't wait," she said, rather glumly.

Epilogue

"Are you sure you don't need me to stay?" Drusilla asked for about the hundredth time. "There's still so much left to do. Work hasn't even started on the Southern Tower. Boggs and I could postpone our trip to the Elfin Isles, just for another week or two."

"Absolutely not," said Ivy, handing Toadstool up to her godmother, who was comfortably tucked between two spines on Elridge's back. "Newlyweds deserve a honeymoon, after all. You and Boggs are no exception. Besides, Elridge is all set to fly you."

"That's right," the dragon agreed cheerfully. "Ivy lent me a book on the Elfin Isles from the castle library, and I can't wait to see the fern forests while I'm there. Do you know the ferns grow to be the size of oak trees?"

"I'm glad you're going to get to enjoy yourself, too," Ivy told the dragon. "You've gone above and beyond your duty as the Dragon Liaison to Ardendale. You've more than earned it."

"And don't worry about the repairs to the castle," said the king, who had joined Ivy, Owen, Tildy, Rose, and Clarinda in the castle garden to see off the happy couple. "Everything's well in hand. By the time you get back, the new southern tower should be close to completed."

Drusilla still looked uncertain. "I don't know. It doesn't feel right to leave with so much still to be done."

"Drusilla, you've worked very hard over the past couple of weeks," said the king. "Helping with the planning and rebuilding, coordinating the workers, chasing those storm clouds away so they didn't impede our efforts."

"Go," urged Ivy. "You deserve it."

"Well...all right," said the fairy, giving Boggs, who was seated behind her, a small smile. "I *have* always wanted to see the Elfin Isles. It's supposed to be one of the most beautiful places in the world."

"I'm sure its beauty pales in comparison to yours, my love," said her husband.

"Oh, Boggs," said Drusilla, giggling. "You're making me blush."

"Are we going to leave sometime today?" Toadstool asked crossly. "At this rate, it'll take us longer to say good-bye then it'll take to get there."

"Toadstool's right. We really should get going." Drusilla patted Toadstool on the head and gave a small wave.

Ivy lingered in the garden longer than the rest of her friends, several minutes after Elridge had lifted into the air. Owen strolled up to stand by her side.

"Drusilla took Toadstool along on their honeymoon?" he asked, watching the dragon fly off into the distance.

"Drusilla said she couldn't bear to be separated from her again," said Ivy, "and I think it's a good thing. Drusilla would only worry about Toadstool otherwise. Besides," she added with a smirk, "it means two whole weeks without listening to Toadstool whine."

"Good point." Owen laughed. Then his face grew serious. "I've been meaning to thank you for what you said to Ninety-Seven back on Jackopia. It was nice of you to stand up for me."

"I meant every word," said Ivy. "Owen, you really are amazingly brave, kind, and clever. I don't know what I'd do without you."

Owen's cheeks flamed. "I've been thinking," he continued, "how many unlikely couples we've seen lately. First, Drusilla and Boggs get married, and then Largessa discovers that Gizzle is her true love. What are the chances?"

"I think it's sweet," said Ivy. "All this romance in the air."

Owen slowly turned to her and cleared his throat, the tips of his ears reddening in that way she found so charming. "You wouldn't think...that perhaps...there's room for more?" he asked shyly. He was so close now, she could almost count the freckles on his nose.

"Definitely," she said, leaning even closer.

High over their heads, the blooms of the meanstalk swayed in the breeze.